Praise for
The Blessing Effect

"After working many years in youth ministry, and now as a Christian music songwriter, I have seen firsthand how words and stories can have an impact on lives. This book provides an antidote to the bullying, violence, and pain that is all too prevalent in our youth today. *The Blessing Effect* shows us that there are no limits when love is put into action."

—ETHAN HULSE, Grammy-nominated,
award-winning songwriter

"Behavioral sciences and Scriptures both reveal the transformative impact that can be achieved from kindness and caring for others. *The Blessing Effect* provides a pragmatic road map for combining acts of kindness and the power of the Holy Spirit. I look forward to seeing how this book will be used to bring about much-needed hope, healing, and restoration in our youth."

—DANA W. SCANNELL, Ph.D., Organizational Psychologist
and Executive Education Instructor at
UCLA Anderson School of Management

"After years leading youth ministry, and now as a men's pastor, I'm excited about how *The Blessing Effect* will be a solid resource for our students and parents. God can use this story to help our kids become the difference makers in their communities."

—TIM LUKEI men's pastor at
ine, California

"I really enjoyed reading *The Blessing Effect* in one sitting. What an amazing story of what you can teach your children every day. Everyone should read this book."
—NICOLE YORKEY of Nicole's Swiss Bliss chocolate treats

"As a father of four teenagers, *The Blessing Effect* vividly captures the challenges and fears this generation faces, as well as providing a powerful remedy through caring for, and engaging others with kindness. Robert puts the power of God, the power of prayer, and the power of encouragement to bring hope to others and ourselves on display."
—KYLE ZIMMERMAN, pastor at
Friends Church in Orange, California

"As an art teacher in the Dallas public school system, I see a real need for my students to read *The Blessing Effect*. This timely and engrossing story needs to be shared today!"
—CYNDY FEASEL, schoolteacher and author of
*After the Cheering Stops: An NFL Wife's Story of
Concussions, Loss, and the Faith That Saw Her Through*

"There is a contagious power that comes from those who put others first. *The Blessing Effect* teaches and encourages us to do just that. What a great way to bring more joy and purpose into the lives of others."
—GREG PATTON, collegiate, U.S. national, and World Team
Tennis head coach and motivational speaker

"I loved working with Robert Pozil on *The Blessing Effect*, which is a wonderful read for families with kids from grade school to high school."
—MIKE YORKEY, author or co-author of more than 100
books, including *The Shot Caller* with Casey Diaz

The Blessing Effect

a novel

by Robert K. Pozil

Print ISBN 978-0-9981687-8-4

Published by Turning Page Books (2nd Edition)

Editorial assistance by Mike Yorkey (mikeyorkey.com)

Cover and interior design by Emily Morelli of Blue Muse Studio (bluemusestudio.com)

To contact Robert Pozil, please visit robertpozil.com

Dedication

Sue, Chris, Katie, Reese, Kelly, and Claire:
you are the inspiration for writing this story,
and because of you . . . I am blessed!

Butterfly Effect: but·ter·fly ef·fect, *noun*

The butterfly effect is the idea that small events can have a large, unpredictable influence on the future.

———————

Blessing Effect: bless·ing ef·fect, *noun*

The blessing effect is the idea that even small amounts of prayer, kindness, and love can have a large and unpredictable influence on one another and the future.

Contents

A Note to the Reader

from Robert K. Pozil

L IFE IS MESSY.
Sometimes, and in some seasons, life gets very messy. This messiness applies to all of us.

Whether you're the popular kid, the loner, a cheerleader, the invisible kid, the star quarterback, a druggie, the smartest one in school, or totally awkward, there are seasons of anxiety, loneliness, or just being uncomfortable in your own skin. No one is immune to these pressures. Because of that, you don't know everything going on in the hearts and minds of others . . . just as others don't really know all the ups and downs, victories and wounds happening deep in your heart.

The fact is that others only see what's on the outside. Sometimes the masks we wear make us look better than we are, and sometimes the masks portray an image that makes us weaker than we feel. Not everything is as it seems, right?

The same is true for your parents. There is no such thing as the Perfect Marriage. Every couple will argue at times or go through periods of tension that cause their own old emotional wounds to resurface. If they are being honest, your parents will tell you that these issues require a lot of attention and effort to make their marriage work and keep the family together.

The adventure you're about to read touches on the raw stuff and simmering tensions that can hit any family, as well as the pain, anxiety, and loneliness that can happen to anyone. I must inform you, however, that this story does not elaborate on all of the difficult challenges with every character. This was done intentionally to place an emphasis on—and highlight—the key message, which is this: Be kind to the people in your life.

The purpose of *The Blessing Effect* is to encourage you to get outside of yourself and to focus on the needs of others. Doing so may be what it takes to radically change the world for the better.

So lean into this challenge. Be courageous. Be bold. Someone may be depending on your kindness to heal—or to unleash the potential buried deep within.

Our world needs you.

Enjoy the journey.

Monday

one

Z ACK TOWERS IS DETERMINED. He has to be. This is
Game 7 of the World Series. There's no tomorrow.
While making his way from the on-deck circle to the
batter's box, he glances at the center field score-
board. The image of his larger-than-life headshot on
the Jumbotron looks supremely confident, and the
stats listed next to his picture confirms his MVP status.

Down by three runs with the bases loaded and two
outs in the bottom of the ninth inning, the capacity
crowd jumps to their feet to cheer their hometown
hero. The deafening cheers echo throughout the packed
stadium and spill out into the parking lot:

Towers, Towers, Towers . . .

With one swing of his mighty bat, Zack can win his team its first World Series championship in franchise history.

As one of baseball's greatest stars readies himself by digging his back foot into the soft dirt of the batter's box and tapping the end of the bat in the middle of the plate, Zack's eyes are poised to pick up the first offering from Pete McNamara, the opponents' star pitcher.

McNamara shakes off one sign, then another. Then, coming out of his windup, the lanky righthander releases a fastball, a 98-mph heater. But to Zack, just as it had happened many times before in situations like this, everything slows down. The pitch seems to be traveling at 45 mph and swells to the size of a Texas grapefruit. As Zack steps into the pitch, his brain makes instantaneous calculations not just to make good contact but to connect with the proper launch angle and deliver a bone-crushing home run that baseball fans will be talking about decades to come.

Just as his favorite bat begins to accelerate, something happens.

Everyone in the stands hears it—a loud, very loud noise that is increasing in volume . . . so loud that Zack's concentration is totally broken as the ball makes its fast approach to the plate. What in the world? What is happening?

"It's 7:30 in the morning, and we're back with your wake-up music mix. The weather is perking up, and we expect a high of 73 degrees by this afternoon . . ."

Not again, Zack thinks. Almost the perfect dream. Almost. He taps his phone to turn off his alarm app and rubs his eyes. He's awake.

Zack rolls out of bed, assuming that he will soon forget "The Dream." As he scans his bedroom floor, he spots a shirt that passes for clean and sort-of-matching pants draped over the back of his desk chair.

Grabbing both, he makes his way for the bathroom. Not just any bathroom, but the only one that he and his younger brother, Tyler, and even his younger sister, Emma, have to share.

There's no time to waste. He has to hurry if he's to have five uninterrupted minutes of quality preparation time. His routine is well-practiced. He showers at night before having dinner and shaves in the morning (about twice per week). Then he washes his face, rubs gel into his hair, and finishes with male-model Zoolander poses in the mirror.

The mirror reveals a view from his upper chest— more developed than the average fifteen-year-old—to his brown-but-not-really-parted hair that presents a sort of brushed-back look to the world. No one would ever believe that he actually spends this much time getting his hair to look like it "fell into place."

Zack heads downstairs to the kitchen, where he grabs a box of Honey Nut Cheerios and places a couple of pieces of wheat berry bread into the toaster. He pours himself a generous bowl of the whole grain cereal, which he douses with milk. Zack is several bites in when his father descends the stairs and joins him at the table.

Dad, known to the rest of the world as Peter Towers, is athletic, fit, and would look a lot younger if he still sported the hair he had back in his college days. Peter takes a seat and bows his head, uttering a quick "Grace." Then he reaches for the box of Cheerios as well.

Neither are in a chatty mood. "Got your homework done?" Peter asks as his oldest son retrieves his toast.

"Think I got it," he replies. Zack pulls a jar of Skippy peanut butter from the fridge.

"Good for you," Peter says. "I hope your brother and sister are getting ready because we have to leave for school soon."

Zack knows that his father has carpool duty. Every other week, Peter drops his kids and their next-door neighbor Justin Anderson, who's Zack's age, off at school. First stop is Emma's elementary school, followed by Tyler's junior high. Then he drops off Zack and Justin at their high school.

As Zack munches on his peanut butter toast while finishing his Cheerios, Tyler and Emma arrive and join them at the table. Zack glances at Tyler, who is twelve and the tallest kid in his class. He wonders how tall Tyler will become . . . and if his younger brother will ever surpass him.

Emma, the youngest and the only girl in the clan, is "all girl." Her light brown hair and blue-green eyes clearly came from her mom, whom her friends call Maggie. Since Emma has spent her entire life competing with her brothers, very few of her nine-year-old classmates can keep up with her in any sport, and that includes the boys.

That Emma is the epitome of a tomboy, Zack thinks. *I wonder what she's going to be like when she grows up?*

— *two* —

MAGGIE IS PREPARING bagged lunches for her three kids, but she knows she is not her usual talkative self. Last night's "disagreement" with Peter seems to have uncharacteristically spilled over to this morning.

Maggie knows that she ought to forgive Peter and move on . . . but she's still playing the mental recording of last night's argument as if it were on a continuous loop. She needs time to process the hurts of the previous night.

Almost without thinking, more like being on auto-pilot, Maggie utters her standard send-off encouragement—"Love you, and be sure to make good choices today"—to the kids as they head out with Peter. The

perfunctory kiss she receives from Peter as he leaves
the house with the kids isn't enough to heal the hurt
from last night.

———————

Peter's first stop is Meyer Street Elementary.

"Hey, Emmer, remember to bless someone today,"
her father says. "You can make someone's day great by
being nice to others."

Emma has heard her father say this so many times
that his words don't mean that much to her. It's kind
of like background noise or just a longer version of her
father saying "Have a good day."

"Okay, Dad, I will. Love you and thanks for the
ride." When Peter drops off Tyler at his junior high, his
instructions are a bit more specific. "Ty, you have been
blessed, so be sure that you reach out to others and be a
blessing to them. I want you to seek out someone, maybe
a kid who looks like he doesn't have any friends and say
hi. Remember: you can change someone's life today."

Tyler chuckles. "Sure, Dad. I'll be sure to do that."

"I love you, Ty!" Peter yells out the window as his
second-oldest son falls in with some friends next to the
Towers' SUV.

Zack notices that Tyler pretends he didn't hear his
father.

Justin, their neighbor, is sitting in the rear bench
seat next to Zack. He leans over and whispers, "Dude,
I'm glad he's not my dad."

Zack rolls his eyes in agreement. He's heard his

father say stuff like this for a long time.

As they approach North Valley High, Zack hears a fluttering sound coming from the engine. The SUV trembles for a second or two—and then the noise disappears as quickly as it came. Back to normal.

That was weird, Zack thinks. Then he turns his attention back to his dad and braces himself for the daily "Tower encouragement."

"Son," his father starts, "you can make a difference today. You can bless someone and end up affecting someone's life. Just think, maybe even Joel. You can change his life by reaching out and blessing him."

Everyone knows that Joel is the angriest kid in school, a real loner. Zack isn't sure what Joel's story is, but Joel isn't part of anything social that's happening at North Valley High. Just about everybody stays out of his way.

His father isn't done yet. "Now imagine that being friendly to Joel helps boost his confidence. Imagine that he gains some self-worth and friends. Then consider what type of person he can become. You see son, you can bless him and impact his life for the better. So reach out to him. Be an agent of love."

Justin and Zack peel out of the SUV and step onto the sidewalk. Zack comes over to the passenger window, which is rolled down.

"Love you, Dad. And hey, you ought to bless someone too."

Zack knows that what he just said might come across as flippant, but he thinks that he's pretty funny.

———————

With no kids left in the car and on his way to work, Peter knows what he has to do. "Hey, Siri. Call Maggie," he tells his phone.

When Maggie answers, Peter starts in. "Hey, baby, I'm sorry for what I said last night and for carrying a grudge. Will you forgive me?"

Maggie sighs. "I was wondering if you would call, but yes, I forgive you. I know we both said some things we regret. I'm sorry too . . . what do you say we move on? We have more important things to focus on."

"Thank you for saying that. I'll do my best to watch what I say. But I want you to know that I love you very much."

Peter realizes he and Maggie don't have a perfect marriage, but they are both aware that any bitterness can become bigger and uglier if not addressed right away. They've learned from previous counseling experiences that forgiveness is a powerful tool for keeping their relationship healthy.

Peter breathes a sigh of relief now that things are back on track. Before they hang up, he has one more question: "Hey, did you sense something up with Zack?"

"I wasn't paying that much attention while I was making their lunches," she answers. "But I do feel like a big decision or important issue is just around the corner for him, but I'm not quite sure what's going on."

"Me too. Kind of a weird unsettling feeling. Let's keep him in our prayers today. Love you."

"Love you too," Maggie says as the call drops off.

Zack arrives at his locker, K225, with just enough time to wave at a few friends and offer "wassups" to several others.

One friend receives a hug, and that's Kelly. She's sort of his girlfriend, but they've never defined their relationship. They seem happy to have more of an emotional connection and deep friendship than anything else.

Kelly's blonde hair and freckles on her petite nose help her blue eyes become her most prominent feature. Her slender five-foot, ten-inch frame is well-suited for volleyball, and she's a starter on the varsity team.

"What's the rush, Zackie?"

"Can't be late for first period, but I'll see you at lunch."

"Sounds like a plan."

Over at Vernon Junior High, Tyler is rushing past the gym to get into the main school building.

The junior high used to be a high school until eight years ago when the new North Valley High was constructed. The benefit to Tyler and the other jocks is that they have a full-size gymnasium and track and field facility.

The gym wall facing the main school building is a solid dark color. Back when the campus was a high school, the gym wall had an impressive mural that showcased the school mascot—a formidable image of a strong tiger. Now that image is hidden beneath many layers of dark paint. But when the sunlight hits the wall just right, and at just the right angle, the faint outline of a tiger can still be seen.

Tyler rushes into his homeroom and plops down in his seat.

The tardy bell rings fifteen seconds later.

Emma is walking through the halls at Meyer Elementary on her way to her classroom. She is just two grades away from being one of the "big kids"—a sixth grader.

She is fairly popular, meaning that older kids sometimes say hello to her or acknowledge her existence. Today she gets some attention from several fifth and sixth graders sitting on the hallway floor outside their classrooms, waiting for their teachers to open the doors and let them in.

Although Emma could get away with wearing dresses and look good in them, she prefers to wear jeans, short-sleeve shirts with slogans like "Too Cute," and retro-style Converse All-Stars. Her Hurley backpack has more than enough room for the few books and notebooks she totes to school each day.

Maggie is preparing for a PTA meeting at her home later that morning. She and eight other women have the privilege of providing input regarding several issues at the elementary school.

Before the gals arrive, Maggie offers up a quick prayer. "Oh, God, I have the sense that Zack is facing a big decision or may be in trouble of some sort. Please let me know how I can pray for him. I sense that he needs You right now. Please protect Zack and let him be filled with Your love."

After finishing with a heartfelt "Amen," she reaches for her second cup of coffee that morning.

Maggie is a youthful-looking forty-year-old mom. Her hair is brown, but unlike Emma, Maggie's hair is straight. Very straight. She looks like she used to be a model, and at five feet, eight inches, the only Towers family member shorter than her is Emma.

As she sips her coffee, she still can't shake the feeling that something is not right with her first-born son.

three

ZACK CAN'T UNDERSTAND it, but for some reason, his dream from earlier in the morning percolates in his subconscious as he walks across the Quad following the lunch bell.

Zack remembers digging his right foot in the batter's box . . . tapping home plate with his bat . . . the fast pitch coming his way . . . the feeling of confidence that he was moments away from hitting a World Series-winning home run in front of millions.

Prior to today, the only times that he remembered his dreams was when he woke up in the morning. The weird thing was that his memory of the dream has not faded away but is actually getting stronger and clearer.

"Hey, you," Kelly calls out. "You alright?"

"Uh, yeah. No problems here," Zack replies as he closes the distance between him and Kelly.

"Are you going to make it to my match after school?"

Zack loves to see her play volleyball, but between his practice sessions in the batting cage and taking care of his younger brother and sister, he had only been able to make it to about half her matches.

"I can't be there for the whole thing, but I should be able to see you make a few blocks and kills in the first set."

"Cool, Zack. I'll make sure to do my best when you're there," she says with a playful smile and a twinkle in her eyes.

They continue chatting as they walk into the Quad— the outdoor bench area for students to eat, hang out, or just do some last-minute prep for a test. They sit down on a bench, where they open their sack lunches. Zack is ravenously hungry and finishes his peanut butter and jelly sandwich in six bites. Then he casts an eye toward Kelly.

"You going to eat that?" Zack points to the remaining half of her turkey and Swiss sandwich.

"Yeah, I am, but you can have a bite."

Zack leans over and bites into her sandwich while Kelly holds it. That feels special to him. Then it happens again—the dream from this morning. He can almost hear the capacity crowd chanting his name . . . *Towers, Towers, Towers* . . . as he steps into the batter's box.

The rich details coming back to him are freaking him out, however. He somehow senses that his dream of winning the World Series, a dream that is his life's ambition, is different now. The confidence to do something great that his parents fostered within him is meant for more than just sports.

But what was he destined for? He wasn't sure. The only thing he *did* know for sure was that there was something different about this morning's dream. And somehow he thought just maybe his life would be different.

"Zack, I don't get you today. You're off in some dream world. You ask for half my sandwich, and then you just sit there looking over at Joel. Do you want him to see you looking at him?"

Zack has no idea that while he was pondering these thoughts, he was unintentionally staring at Joel, the kid in black. Joel is sitting with no one next to him, probably by his choice, and just about everyone else's choice. Very few people would dare to sit near him.

"Sorry 'bout that. You remember a long time ago when I told you about my home run dream. Well, I had it again last night."

"But you said that dream was the best feeling ever. So why do you look so . . . like you just failed a math final?"

"Don't know."

They continue chatting until the lunch-ending bell rings. When Kelly slings her backpack on, Zack spots a look on Kelly's face that says, *I sure hope you make it to the start of my match.*

As they prepare to leave the Quad for their afternoon classes, he files the lingering thoughts about his morning dream away, like storing books in his locker. Out of sight, out of mind.

He hopes.

As most of the students walk to class, Zack is sensing something deep within. He has felt this type of thing a couple of times before.

Once at church when he stood up and responded to an altar call and committed his life to God. Another time was when his parents took him to a soup kitchen, where he mingled with other kids, thinking they were there to help out too, only to find out that those teens were part of the homeless crowd.

On those occasions, he felt connected to something bigger than himself, like life had more meaning than hitting a walk-off home run.

The dream momentarily flashes in his mind again. Wasn't his dream supposed to be securely locked away? Whatever happened to "out of sight, out of mind"?

Then, to make matters worse, his dad's send-off echoes in his mind: *Remember to bless someone.*

What about Joel?

Zack doesn't want to go there. *Oh crap, I know I should approach Joel, but I really don't want to. He seems so freaky.*

One thing Zack knows: these kinds of thoughts make him uncomfortable.

And that's not a good thing.

—— *four* ——

JOEL, ALSO A sophomore, is fifteen, the same age as Zack. It wasn't that long ago when they were friends, even though they didn't hang out too often.

Joel used to have curly brown hair and a hang-loose surfer look. Now his hair is straight and jet black, parted to the side and flat against his forehead. He likes to paint his fingernails in different colors just to make a statement.

His wardrobe consists of black skinny jeans, ripped and distressed at the knees, a black T-shirt emblazoned with **Don't Think Too Much** in white lettering, a black ballcap without a logo, and Lugz sneakers, also in black. The evidence of cryptic tattoos can be seen running down the inside of his right forearm and can almost be seen on the left side of his neck just above his shirt collar. A silver piercing curls around his left nostril. Two silver necklaces of varied lengths dangle from his neck.

Zack knows there are plenty of kids who are lonely, nerdy, and even depressed who look pretty normal and wouldn't be so intimidating to approach, but Joel is in a league of his own. So why would his dad tell him to bless Joel? And why today? Zack's already freaking out about his dream, which came out of nowhere just before the alarm went off.

A buddy from American History class making his way from the Quad to the main building passes in front of him. "Yo, Z-Man, why aren't you movin' quicker to get your butt to class?"

Zack grunts. Not that Corey really cares about his academic status. This was just his way of saying hi.

"Glad to see you too buddy. Just thinking about things and not totally with it today. You know?"

"Whatever dude. Save the soft stuff for Kelly. Anyways, you going to the volleyball match today?"

"Just the beginning. Can't stay for the whole thing. Tyler and Emma will be home and my mom has to step out . . . so she wants me home by five o'clock."

The entire time, Zack is glad to be talking so he doesn't have to be inside his head. It feels safer to be talking and not thinking.

"Sure, Captain."

Although Zack being one of the captains on the varsity baseball team as a sophomore is an honor, the way Corey says it makes it sound more like Zack is a "teacher's pet" rather than one of the best players in the conference.

"Very funny, Corey. You'll be lucky to even play a couple innings per game since you'll be riding the pine!" The zinger prompts Corey to change the subject.

"Zack, you see the new girl? Did you catch her name?" Although Corey is popular with the girls, the way his voice squeaks reveals his nervousness about approaching the new girl in the school.

"Dude, oh, my *little* friend, since when are you nervous about girls?" Zack teases, even though he and Corey are the same height.

"No, it's just th-th-thaaaat she's so good looking. I mean, she, she, she's hot."

Even Corey is laughing a bit. His stuttering gives away that he is crushing on the new girl.

Zack has an immediate solution. "Why don't you accidentally find a way to bump into her after next period and ask her to come with you to the volleyball match? You can tell her that it would be a great way to meet some people."

"Z-Man, you're alright." Corey initiates what looks like a high five but it evolves into a roundhouse clap, kind of like a slap at the 12 o'clock position and then meeting up again at six o'clock, followed by another orchestrated hand slap/handshake and ending with something that sounds like "Ohhh, yeah!"

With that, Corey whistles as he walks to class with the confidence of a World Series-winning home run strut. Zack knows exactly what Corey's thinking and how his friend will come up with a "coincidental" meeting with that beautiful girl who left him tongue-tied.

————————

Zack is so happy to have a normal, shallow conversation that he's startled by the jolt that brings him back to his contemplative mood.

Your blessing Joel could affect him in a profound way. Reach out to him . . .

His father's word echo like a gong in his mind. Zack is not sure if his dad's words come from his mind, or from somewhere else. Perhaps from his heart.

Then it happens. Time stops, or perhaps the bite of turkey and Swiss sandwich had some old mayonnaise that's freaking out his system. One thing he knows for sure, there's no way he's ever felt like this before.

Still in the Quad, he looks around but can't see another person. Then he listens intently, realizing the silence is so strong that he can almost hear the nothingness. Zack senses someone is behind him, but he's too afraid to turn around. He's not even sure if he's tracking time accurately.

Is this all happening to him in a span of seconds or minutes—or longer? He can't tell.

Get a hold of yourself Zack. Quit psyching yourself out. It was just one nasty sandwich that's not sitting right, and you're still tripping about the dream thing. C'mon, take a breath and calm down.

Zack does his best to relax and rid himself of the fear. But he is still tripping out, and to add to his uneasiness, now feels like someone, or something, is right behind him. He knows that he has to find out who or what it is.

With that, Zack turns to his left, but just his head. His eyes do not want to see what is behind him, so as his head turns left, his eyes rotate away to avoid the inevitable as long as possible. Slowly the eyes make the commitment to see what is lurking behind him, just out of his sight.

"What in the . . ."

Zack cannot get the words out.

Maggie picks up her cell phone.

"Do you want to meet for lunch today?" Peter asks.

Maggie doesn't have to be asked twice. "Sounds good to me. In fact, I was just getting ready to call you to ask the same thing. I have a lot on my heart and want to talk with you."

Maggie knows she is the key to Peter's world. She is not only his lover, but the two of them exude true synergy. The result of their partnership and friendship helps them be better people. Friends say that when they are around her and Peter, they come away feeling energized or sometimes filled with joy. Today, Peter and Maggie need to get that from each other.

"Let's meet up at the Mexican place you like," Maggie offers. She is well aware that Mexican food has a way of putting Peter in the best of moods.

"You're on. See you in fifteen minutes."

They arrive at Eduardo's restaurant at the same

time, even parking next to each other. Peter and Maggie greet one another with a quick kiss and hug, then hold hands as they walk into Eduardo's together. The hostess seats them at an outdoor table, which meets with Maggie's approval. Outdoors is a fine environment to talk about the things on their hearts.

Peter beckons her to take first from a bowl of warm tortilla chips placed on the table. She dips a chip into the mild salsa and takes a crunchy bite.

"Remember when you asked me about Zack this morning?" she begins, reaching for a second triangular-shaped chip with grains of salt. "Well, I was praying for him this morning and got the sense that he needed our prayers for strength to make a right decision. Does that mean anything to you?"

Peter mulls his answer as he finishes chewing on his first tortilla chip. "Yes and no. I know how you feel because I sense that something is up too. But I can't put my finger on it. I'm not sure if he is in danger or being challenged with something."

Maggie knows her husband was almost never concerned in a scared type of way for Zack, but his voice reveals a concern for wanting to protect his son.

Maggie inhales then exhales a calming breath. "Peter, we know that Zack is a good kid and makes good choices," recalling how she sends the kids off to school. "You know," she continues, "just talking with you is confirming my hunch that something may be going on with Zack."

"Yeah, I know what you mean. After dropping Zack off, I felt like I should stop and pray for him, it's like I was compelled to lean on God at that moment . . . like really look to Him for guidance."

Maggie suddenly experiences a hunger for prayer, a hunger more real than anyone's hankering for an epic burrito. "How about we pray now?" she asks.

Peter nods. He reaches for Maggie's hand and bows his head as she starts to pray. When she is finished, Peter is in full agreement, and then continues, "God, we trust You with our son and thank You for protecting him. We thank You for Your presence that is even now surrounding him and filling him with Your power. We know that You have Your hedge of protection around him, and we thank You for that. Help Zack to see with his heart and to be open to Your guiding, to be open to Your plan for this day, for his life."

Maggie and Peter, in sync with each other, offer a heartfelt and faith-filled "In Jesus' name, amen."

"Everything okay?"

Maggie opens her eyes and looks at their server. Her name tag says Marlena.

"That's very nice of you to ask."

Maggie recognizes her from past visits to Eduardo's. "We're just fine, Marlena. You know kids, they always keep us on our knees, right?

"Got two of my own," says the server. "It's nice to hear you praying for your son."

five

At Meyer Street Elementary School, Emma senses that her fourth grade desk mate, Vickie, is unsuccessful in searching for something.

Each of the twelve desks in the classroom are wide enough for two kids to sit side by side, with each having their own compartment just under the desk to hold pencils, erasers, and other oft-needed fourth grader items. Emma knows that Vickie comes from a family that immigrated from Korea, and ever since the first grade, they've been good friends. About once a month, they have a sleepover.

Vickie's short black bangs are clutched tightly in her hands. She looks frustrated, like she can't figure something out.

"What?" Emma leans over to Vickie, mostly pushing her ear toward Vickie but keeping her head straight ahead so that it won't be so obvious to Mrs. Cranston that they're talking.

"I had my pencil all ready for this test we have to take, but I can't find it now," Vickie whispers in a strained voice.

"No biggie, Vickie, just use this." Emma hands an extra No. 2 from her under-the-desk cubby.

"Really? Thanks!" Vickie whispers back, but her smile seems forced.

Emma knows her friend, and she can tell something else is still bothering her.

Zack isn't sure what he's looking at.

It was definitely a man. No, not a man. More like a hologram. No, not a hologram. More like a large man that was somehow radiating light, or glowing. Zack can't move a muscle. He is terrified.

"This lunch is just what I needed, baby."

"Me too," Maggie replies. "Whatever challenge Zack may be facing, I know that we just did exactly what we needed to do—pray and then trust God. Let's continue to keep Zack in our prayers throughout the day."

"Sounds like a great plan. And hey, I love you, baby!"

With that, they make their way to their cars, and with a quick kiss and a smile, they each take off in opposite directions.

———————

Zack thinks that he should run, and run fast. He wants to get inside the main building and find a teacher, someone in authority, or just any adult. What he really wants is to be anywhere this glowing dude is not.

The large man, or whatever it is, has blond hair to his shoulders and looks like he belongs on a Viking ship from a thousand years ago. He must be six feet, six inches, but he looks taller because of his massively broad shoulders and muscular—but not muscle-bound—physique.

Zack cannot figure out what the clothes are all about. He wears a long buttonless, loose-fitting shirt that nearly reaches his knees. The white shirt is tight to his waist with a wide leather belt. Leather sandals adorn his feet, but they are different than he's ever seen in person before. The sandals resemble what Roman soldiers would wear in films like *Gladiator* and *Ben-Hur*. His face is without hair and his blue eyes glisten against his bronze-toned skin.

Zack is not sure if the man or thing, or whatever it is, is mad or not. He only knows that he dons a serious look on his face.

———————

At Vernon Junior High, Tyler is such a prankster that no one knows when to take him seriously. Despite his constant joking around, he is the best student in his family. His older brother and younger sister earn a report card filled with pretty much B's, but Tyler is always bringing home A's.

He's almost as good as Zack in sports. But Tyler prefers acting silly and getting people to laugh rather than working hard by doing stuff like taking extra batting practice or fielding ground balls, which is something that his big brother, Zack, has endless energy to do.

Nearly everyone at the junior high seems to know Tyler's older brother, and most people think Tyler and Zack look alike. Except for some similar attributes—their build, their smiles, and their last name—they're quite different looking.

Tyler has softer facial features, and his dark hair is more wavy and longer than Zack's. Unlike the ambiguity of Zack's doo, Tyler's is confidently parted to the side. Tyler's eyes are hazel, while Zack's are greenish-blue.

After passing through the cafeteria line, Tyler is making his way to the Cool Table, tray in hand. He spots a kid he never really noticed before sitting by himself.

"What's your name?" Tyler asks.

"Uh . . . Harold. Why?"

"Well, if you're just sitting by yourself, why don't you grab your tray and come sit with us?"

"What? Me?"

Tyler can see that Harold is nervous and scared. Harold seems like the kind of kid who's twitchy all the time. Then Tyler glances over Harold's shoulder, where his "cool" friends are sitting. They're giving Tyler looks that say, *What are you doing? Don't do it, dude! Leave him there!*

Tyler performs the calculus in his mind and realizes there is no way out. *Oh, crap. I guess I'm in too deep now.* He looks to Harold. "Yes, you. How about you bringing your stuff and sitting with me and the guys over there."

Tyler realizes that he's probably sounding incredibly insincere, like the time he told his grandmother that the reindeer sweater she gave him for Christmas was just what he wanted.

Nonetheless, with trays in hand, the two boys approach the Cool Table.

"Bill, Mike, Fluff, Jake, and Peter, this is um . . . this is Harold. Harold, these are the guys. Fluff's real name is James, but you can see why we call him Fluff because of his crazy hair."

A chorus of lackluster "Heys" come back, along with a few head nods. A couple of the guys don't even bother to make eye contact—like the way they'd avoid looking at their teacher when trying not to get called on in class.

Tyler makes room for Harold and asks the newbie some basics about himself. Turns out that he wasn't a jock, which was a prerequisite for gaining a permanent seat at the Cool Table, but he did have a phenomenal knowledge of their favorite bands. And, for a few of the kids just learning guitar, they were impressed that Harold seemed to be a master guitarist.

"Hey, do any of you guys want to play my Fender guitar with me sometime?" Harold blurts out awkwardly. "I have an extra one with an extra amp and pedals."

Bill is the most excited by the offer. "That sounds pretty cool. Fender, huh? I'm in."

Tyler notices how Harold exhales a sigh of relief. He's glad that the guys, who would usually look for ways to mock newcomers or put them in their place, cut Harold a little slack.

Tyler is wearing a smile. He's feeling good about how this is all playing out.

six

"WHY DID YOU delay? Did you not know that this was your assignment?"

Zack stares at the large Scandinavian-looking man. His words sound like a rushing river spilling over the falls. His lips move when he talks, but the power and sound are more than just words.

"Who are you?" Zack is trembling. He flutters like the SUV's engine that morning . . . but for Zack, it doesn't go away after a few seconds.

"My name is Ashkah, and I have been sent by the Holy One, the One Who Is That He Is. I am merely a messenger from the Master."

Zack has questions, but he can't speak. He has to sit

down, so he takes a spot on a lunch bench in the Quad to gather himself.

Great. Now I know I've lost it. I've got a giant Viking man talking to me.

As if reading his mind, Ashkah addresses him. "This is more real than anything you have ever known. You will be given a gift today to see what could come to pass."

Zack is keenly aware of Ashkah's ultra-serious countenance.

With that, the Mighty Messenger comes over to Zack and helps him to his feet. Weird feelings change quickly within Zack's gut, from fear and confusion to peace and calm. It happens at the precise moment the large being touches him.

In a split second, Zack experiences a burst of reality: How will he make it on time to his next class? What will his teachers say when they see a massive, strangely dressed man accompanying him in the classroom?

They walk together away from the Quad and head toward a two-story brick building that houses most of the classrooms and all of the administration offices. As they enter the building, Zack glances at the clock on the wall.

The hands say 2:45. That can't be right. It's only 12:30.

Zack pulls his phone from his right pocket. The time on the wall is correct, it's 2:45.

Zack turns to Ashkah, and the messenger affirms with a nod that conveys *Yes, it's quarter to three.*

Zack looks into the classroom to his left, and the door is open.

Sitting in the middle of the class is Kelly. She's looking out the open door the moment he passes by, like she is waiting to see him.

Zack stops and smiles.

She doesn't return the smile or respond at all, almost like she's ignoring him.

She must be mad at me because of the lunch thing, he thinks. *Or maybe she's tripping out about my oversized escort.* Zack has total clarity of mind, but somehow not everything is in focus.

Ashkah gives him a look, says nothing, but doesn't take his eyes off of Zack, who senses that somehow they are navigating the halls unseen.

As quickly as his concern shifted to Kelly, though, it shifts back to Ashkah.

"Zack, I have been sent as a messenger for you this day. I am from the Most High God. See with your heart and understand that I will show you things that He wants you to know."

A simple, yet firm command comes from his messenger, "Come."

Zack is so unsure of his physical body that he swears that they just passed through a wall of lockers, like they were "cutting a corner" to save time and quickly get to the adjacent hall.

What the . . . Did I just walk through lockers-wall-lockers as we cut the corner and made our way to the intersecting hallway?

Zack reaches for his phone again to see if time is slipping away. Not at all. The time is 2:52.

On the playground during lunch, Emma examines a look on Vickie's face that is not her typical carefree expression.

"Something wrong, Vickie? What's up?"

"If you come to the swings with me, we can talk, okay?"

Two seats are empty next to each other. Not a rare thing, but a pleasant surprise for the girls. They each select their swing and begin the lean-back, legs-out, tilt-legs, forward-tuck routine.

Once they reach their cruising altitude, Vickie asks, "Hey, Emma, do you ever get scared?"

"Sure. Doesn't everybody get scared sometimes?"

"Do your parents ever fight? I mean, like really yell at each other?"

Emma wasn't expecting that question. She wonders if Vickie is hoping for a yes by the way she asked it.

"Sometimes they get mad and raise their voices and say stuff, but they usually make up pretty fast. Except for last night. I heard them yelling but couldn't make out what they were saying. They were mad at each other, though. Then this morning, I could tell that they were still upset. Why do you ask?"

"Well, my mom and dad were fighting in their bedroom last night, too, and I thought I heard them say that they should get a divorce. I'm totally freaking out about it. I don't want my parents to split up. I just want them to stop fighting. I mean, what's so hard about that? Why can't they stop fighting?"

They come to a standstill on the swings. Emma can tell that Vickie is being brave and holding back tears. She wants to help her friend.

"My mom always tells me to pray when things are tough. In fact, she even tells me to pray when things are good."

Emma doesn't mean to come across as funny, but the comment strikes Vickie's funny bone. She chuckles, which lowers the tension, then flashes a smile that suggests she feels good about praying.

Emma wants to help. "If you want, I can pray for you and ask God to help your parents to get along and that their marriage can be better."

"Um . . . okay."

Emma bows her head and closes her eyes, but she sneaks a peek to see if Vickie has closed her eyes. She has. Emma clears her throat and begins praying out loud.

"God, please help Vickie's parents to get along and stop fighting," she prays. "That would mean so much to my friend. Amen."

Emma looks at Vickie. She doesn't look as scared or worried as she did just before the quick prayer.

"Thanks," Vickie whispers to Emma.

"Of course!" Emma says a bit louder than Vickie's whisper.

Emma begins swinging again. "What do you say we try to get as high as we can."

"You're on," Vickie replies.

seven

As Ashkah walks faster and faster, almost at a brisk jog, Zack keeps up but he can't understand the hurry.

"You must understand," Ashkah declares.

Reading my mind again. "Okay, I'll try, but what's going on?"

Ashkah does not answer, but the messenger gives Zack a serious look that pierces his eyes, then through them. At that moment, Zack catches a glimpse of Ashkah's eyes. For the first time, he realizes that the driving force behind Ashkah is love. A firm and tough love, but definitely love.

"Stop," the messenger says.

Ashkah stops so abruptly that Zack nearly trips over him as he tries to come to a halt next to the large man.

"Here. Wait."

Zack looks at his watch: 2:59.

The next sixty seconds take forever. Right at 3 o'clock, though, time accelerates back to normal pace with sounds, commotion, and energy moving at full speed again. Doors fling open. Students exit their classrooms and flood the hallway. Lockers open and close. Backpacks go in and out of lockers. Loud and excited voices taste their afternoon freedom.

Then it happens. Breaking the noise like a rock shattering a window, an explosion erupts that's so loud it breaks, no, destroys the background hum of carefree chatter.

Zack feels the blast go past him. Actually, the blast goes *through* him. He knows exactly where he is—near Kelly's locker. He needs to find her.

Zack screams. "No!" Then his mouth and limbs go numb as the reality of the last moment settles inside his mind: the explosion came from Kelly's locker!

The hallway is mayhem, a madhouse of chaos and screams. Students stampede in every direction. Zack takes three closer steps to check on Kelly.

Is she there? Is she okay?

And then he sees her, splayed on the ground, unconscious. Blood has soaked her clothes, shredded by the explosion. Her left hand appears to be dangling from her wrist. Zack doesn't know anything about triaging, but even he can tell she's in bad shape from an explosive device that someone had planted in her locker.

She didn't look like the same Kelly that he had enjoyed lunch with a few hours earlier. She lays motionless on the ground in front of the mangled metal that used to be her locker.

Zack gets close enough to stand over her. He loves her, but also knows that her life will never be the same. Will she even live?

Then a second explosion rocks the building but comes from the hallway around the corner.

What? That's where he and Ashkah had cut the corner just minutes earlier. Within seconds, more smoke and screams fill the air. He doesn't want to leave Kelly. He needs to stay with her. But he is being pulled away against his will and being drawn to investigate the next explosion.

As panicking students sprint past him, he and his messenger backtrack and make their way effortlessly through the crowd and toward the second tragedy. Amid the pandemonium, Zack is now aware of sounds of sirens as teachers, P.E. coaches, and other adults try to gain some sense of order and evacuation. Even the adults look totally rattled.

When Zack arrives, he's stunned to see a second victim. It's Corey, laying still and lifeless in a pool of his blood in front of a locker that exploded in his face. It's apparent that when the device triggered, the locker door ripped right into him. Point blank. Nothing to slow down or deflect the shrapnel.

Zack thinks about how, just moments before, Corey was so excited to meet that new girl. He was probably thinking about what he was going to say to her when they sat next to each other at the volleyball match at the moment that the metal particles penetrated his torso and head.

"No way, no way, no way, no way," is all that Zack can utter as he gazes down at Corey.

Ashkah places his hand on Zack's shoulder. "We're not done yet," he says.

Zack can't take anymore. He is spinning. He is numb—like a zombie.

They walk past the carnage as kids and faculty exit the main building and head outside in the direction of the Quad. Still in the hallway, Ashkah takes Zack to the janitor's closet next to the Boy's bathroom. The closet looks like another classroom because it has the same type of door as any other class, even a number: **103**.

As they approach, Zack hears someone say, "Don't chicken out now. Do it. Do it."

No one else is inside this part of the building, and there's an eerie silence that contrasts the noise of just a few minutes ago. The only sounds are a lone male voice coming from inside the janitor's closet—and the sound of Zack's racing heart.

Zack must investigate. He opens the door to Room 103.

Bang! Such a piercing and loud sound! Too loud for his ears, which haven't fully recovered from the first two explosions. Once again, his ears ring. And ring some more.

It's Joel. Zack opens the door just in time to see Joel place the barrel of the handgun against his forehead and pull the trigger. In an instant, from an almost military looking, saluting position, he collapses. His legs turn to Jell-O, then his upper body follows in one descending lifeless motion—like air escaping out of a life-size balloon.

Zack spots a notebook on the floor. A pair of pages fall open. From where he's standing, Zack can see a list of numbers—locker numbers.

KELLY K284 24-13-18

COREY K207 12-19-26

ZACK K225 17-22-20

Next to the notebook is a bag with Zack's name on it. What looks to be another explosive device protrudes from the bag. Literally.

Ashkah nods to Zack. "Go!"

Zack begins running, driven partly by fear, partly by following instructions. He's running *hard*.

By the time he makes it to the Quad, the place is deserted with the exception of official-looking people doing official-looking things.

Zack sits on his bench, the familiar bench—the same one that he and Kelly shared earlier in the day. With his head in his hands, palms covering his eyes, he absentmindedly mutters, "God, I do not understand . . . I can't understand. Why? *Why?*"

It seems like an eternity that Zack is sitting, grieving, exhausted, spent, done. Time does not have any meaning, and it's impossible to know how long he's been occupying the bench. The destruction, death, and chaos weigh Zack with the heaviness of an anvil that pushes him deeper into the bench.

Zack is immobilized by the weight. He sits and sits and sits. How much time elapses? It can't be measured. Like trying to measure a sunrise or a sunset.

So Zack just sits. After an eternity on the bench, he begins to feel the sun shining through his hands and slightly warming his face. He also feels the familiar warmth of the day that had evaded him ever since he met Ashkah.

Zack has seen too much. Lost too much. He is sure that he will not enjoy life like he has in the past . . . not with the heavy anvil of grief and loss overloading him.

His ears are still ringing from Joel's fatal shot. But he is also beginning to hear nearby voices.

————————

"What in the world is your deal? I'm not going to ask you again. Are you going to have a bite of my sandwich or not?"

Zack raises his head slowly, fighting gravity, but he isn't ready to open his eyes yet. He has been in a war zone. He just lost the girl he loved. He knew initially that she had been badly hurt, but when he'd seen her taken away in the stretcher with the sheet completely covering her, he realized that she was gone, gone forever . . . and that he really did love her.

Who can be nagging him about eating a sandwich at a time like this? What does this person want? Zack is too spent to think.

He slowly opens his eyes, but like exiting a movie theater in the middle of the afternoon, his eyes are not ready to adjust to the bright sunlight.

"What?" Zack asks, squinting his eyes and with a combination of annoyance and bewilderment in his voice.

"That's it. I'm eating it myself," Kelly says with defiance and a smile.

Zack peels a look at his watch. It's 12:20. His heart races.

"What are you doing here?" Zack is not aware that he still has the capacity for being stunned today. He is both exhausted and energized at the same time.

"Zack Towers, I'm not sure what I see in you. Well, besides the fact that you're really cute."

Zack isn't paying attention to Kelly's words—he's too elated. "Hey, Kelly, it's 12:20. It's 12:20. And look! There's Corey over there with Chad!"

Zack's voice squeaks at an octave higher than normal. A burst of adrenaline rushes through him.

"Okay, you win. You are definitely the biggest goof ball of the day."

Zack stands up and looks at Kelly for some time. Just looking into her eyes and then from her head to her toes. He embraces her with a long hug. At first, it's just him hugging her because her arms lie straight against her side. But as he presses her more closely, her arms are finally liberated and reach around Zack to return the warm embrace.

"Hey, Kelly. You know that sometimes I ask you to pray for me. Well, now is a really good time. I've got something that must be done."

Joel sits motionless on the rock, which serves as his lone eating station.

"Hey, Joel."

In the past, Zack would have never approached Joel. But after what he saw, he knows what he has to do.

eight

JOEL LOOKS AT Zack, but Joel's eyes reject him. The bitterness and anger brewing deep within leak out of his eyes and spill over into Zack's direction.

In a flash, Joel experiences a slideshow of hurtful events that sequentially span several years. Events such as not being invited to parties . . . being left out of conversations . . . being laughed at to his face. Even in the rapid-fire succession of images, feelings, and memories flooding his zone, it's not clear to Joel if he is the target of all the ridicule, but it hurts nonetheless.

Meanwhile, the slideshow continues: being ignored in class . . . being unwanted in the hallways . . . and being untouched by girls. That's what being all alone in this world feels like.

Then, in the expansion of this time-standing-still second, he can see images of Zack, Corey, and Kelly. They are carefree. They belong and are accepted by others. Their lives seem just too easy. In this fourth-dimension moment, he is acutely aware of his feelings.

This isn't fair. He hates those who rejected him. He wants them punished. They must be the root cause of his misery and loneliness.

Because of that, it's their fault. They deserve retribution.

"Joel, it's been a while, huh?"

"Been a while since what, Towers?'"

Zack is not at all surprised but is just a bit taken back by the reality and vehemence of Joel's words, which are void of any emotion. All the more reason to love on him.

"Been a while since we've talked," Zack replies. He's experiencing a confidence that's reminiscent of the feeling in his dream when the fastball seemed to slow down while increasing in size. "Look, I saw you sitting here, and thought that maybe you would, um . . . I don't know. Maybe you and I can talk. You know, not about anything special, just talk."

Zack does something he wouldn't have done yesterday. He places his hand on Joel's shoulder.

Joel is nervous.

He's experiencing emotion, something he's not used to.

So why is Zack placing a hand on his shoulder?

Zack silently asks the Lord for help.

Zack picks up on Joel recoiling. His movement isn't fast, just a slow shrug to regain his isolation. Zack sits on a rock that's just large enough for two, yet low enough so their feet easily reach the ground. With Zack sitting to Joel's right, they are almost shoulder-to-shoulder.

You get to bless Joel today and make an impact that will affect many.

Zack hears these words in his heart, but it isn't an echo of what his father said to him that morning . . . this time it sounds like Ashkah's voice. The words feel like refreshing water for a parched mouth. A tremendous peace permeates all of Zack's being. The same peace he experienced at the altar call. The same peace he experienced at the soup kitchen. Peace.

"I remember when I used to see you go surfing in the early mornings before school, back in what—fifth or sixth grade?" Zack asks, recalling a memory that pops into his mind.

"Dude, you are so off. I can't believe that you came over here to ask me about surfing." Joel pauses, a long pause, then adds with annoyance in his tone, "It was sixth grade."

"You were good in the water. I used to watch you

during the summer competitions. Do you miss surfing?"

"Towers . . . ." Joel looks at him, not in the eyes, but just below Zack's chin. *That was the best time of my life,* Joel thinks to himself. Then lifting his head, he expresses his defiance out loud for Zack, saying in a cutting cadence, "So what do you want?"

"Nothing," Zack offers. "I don't know. I guess I figured that you'd be a surfer forever."

Joel's breath quickens as he thinks to himself, *Me too.* Then with a smirk he mutters, "Whatever."

Zack has an idea. "Hey, would you like to go out to The Point with me? I kinda suck at surfing, but the waves are supposed to be pretty good this week. We could do a session before school tomorrow."

"Why would you want to hit the waves with me? You haven't talked to me or looked at me without laughing since I don't know when. I see you and Blondie and that Corey kid. I know the crap you say about me."

Zack isn't sure how to respond. Then he hears in his heart the following words: *Ask for forgiveness.*

Feeling it's the right thing to do, he addresses Joel with the following question: "Will you forgive me?"

"What?" Joel asks with a mixture of anger, bewilderment, and confusion.

Zack's question momentarily stuns Joel. In his mind, there's no question that Zack, Kelly, and Corey had hurt him badly over the years. Joel replays the mental tape of the three of them looking and gawking at him . . .

and then laughing. Their mocking left deep wounds and scars, causing Joel to hide deeper and deeper behind his dark facade. He figured that if he built a wall high enough and thick enough, no one could penetrate him. No one could hurt him. Then he would be safe, even though that meant that he would go through life isolated and lonely. This is just a part of what got him lost in his anger, bitterness—and alone.

Zack takes a step closer. "Please forgive me for how we, I mean I, treated you."

"You're asking me for forgiveness? That's rich. If you only knew."

Joel gives Zack the "I know something you don't know" look.

Be attentive. Everything you were shown today—the destruction and pain—was the product of Joel's imagination. He entertained those thoughts in his mind and heart.

Ashkah's voice is strong yet compassionate.

Zack speaks up again. "But guess what? I do know."

"Know what Towers?" Joel mumbles as he exhales. "You're insane!" he declares with forcefulness.

With calm, confidence, and peace filling his body, an unrattled Zack turns his head and looks straight at Joel. "I know all about your thoughts of getting even with the people who hurt you. The list of locker numbers in your spiral notebook, the explosives in the lockers, the janitor's room, the gun." Zack's voice is steady and not judgmental.

Joel panics. "What are you talking about Towers?"

"You know, the devastation you thought about. Everything. I know all about it. Listen, I don't know how to explain this to you, but Joel, I know."

Zack sees that Joel is in shock. He had been in his own world for so long. The walls have been breached, and Joel's secret isn't a secret anymore.

This is crazy. How could Zack know all that stuff, Joel wonders.

The breach is totally freaking him out. His head is spinning.

"Why are you doing this?" Joel asks, catching his breath.

"Because I know your heart, and I remember the Joel of sixth grade. And so do you."

"Zack, I don't know what to say."

Zack notices that this is the first time Joel doesn't refer to him as Towers.

Joel continues, "You come over to my space and ask me to forgive you for being a jerk for who knows how long. Then you tell me about some revenge stuff that I'm supposedly thinking about. I don't know, man."

With a sense of boldness and confidence, Zack makes

him a stunning offer, "Why don't you come with me after school? I'm stopping by the volleyball match for the first twenty minutes or so, then I have to go home to watch Ty and Emma. We can hang at my house . . . and you can just let me know later if you'd like to surf tomorrow."

Joel is doing some serious thinking. In this moment, he realizes that he would never really want to hurt others or die from his own hand. It's just that the anger, emotional wounds and loneliness had piled up and burdened him so greatly that erasing the pain felt like an option.

Now, Zack is acting friendly to him, a social leper. A bit of the heaviness in his heart lifts, like taking away a five-pound bag from a wheelbarrow filled with three dozen five-pound bags. Does that make a noticeable difference? It does a little, and Joel almost hears himself saying yes to Zack's invitation, but he isn't quite ready.

"I don't know. Maybe," he says.

nine

As Maggie drives away from Eduardo's, she has a glow on her face that reflects what she feels deep within her heart that at that moment, Zack is making good choices. She just feels it. She senses God's peace is upon him and that he is in the protection of the Almighty.

"Thank you, Lord," she says out loud in the direction of the sunroof. A weight in her heart is lifting. She is smiling.

"Hey, Zack! Can I talk to you for a minute?" Kelly's sweet

voice reaches all the way across the Quad, where Zack and Joel are sitting next to each other. Zack notices that his ears are no longer buzzing from the blasts and gunshot he heard—or had he really experienced that horrible mayhem?

"Yup. Just a sec," he says in a loud enough voice so Kelly can hear him across the Quad. Turning back to Joel, Zack continues their conversation.

"Hey, I know that this all seems too crazy, and I'm tripping about this too. How about this . . . we meet up outside Sheffield's classroom after sixth, come with me to watch Kelly play volleyball, then we'll head to my house. You know, we can just chill at my place for a bit. What do you say?"

Zack meets Joel's gaze and can see that Joel is still processing things. Maybe too much stuff to absorb. It's a lot to take in for both of them. And then, after a thoughtful pause, Joel gives the slightest nod and heads towards his next class.

I sure hope that Joel meets up with me after sixth period, Zack half-thinks, half-prays as he makes his way toward Kelly.

———

As Tyler is leaving school, he walks out the front doors and down a walkway that leads to the sidewalk, where he waits for his buddy Mike Meyers, who lives just six houses past the Towers' place. They walk home together after school nearly every day.

When Tyler arrives at their usual meeting spot,

he notices Harold getting a ride home with his mom. Harold hops into the front seat of a blue minivan as Mike approaches Tyler.

Tyler greets Mike, then turns and makes eye contact with Harold.

"Hey, Harold," Tyler yells out, "See you later."

Harold is still wearing a goofy grin and is almost too giddy to reply. He rolls down the window and shouts, "Okay," just before his mom begins to pull away.

As the blue minivan drives off, Tyler is pretty sure that he overhears Harold telling his mother, "See, Mom? That's the cool guy I was just telling you about."

———

While still in her car, Maggie receives a phone call on her Bluetooth connection. It's Peter.

As soon as she answers, Peter asks, "Hey, Maggie, I still have Zack on my mind. How about you?"

"Weird that you would call right now. I was just feeling a sense of peace and the Lord's protection on Zack. Not sure I can explain it, but I just have this sense that he's okay."

Maggie wants to say that she has an impression that something supernatural is going on with Zack, but she isn't sure how to explain the thought or even say it without sounding crazy. Maybe she can find the right words when they see each other later that night.

———

At the North Valley High volleyball match, Joel is sitting next to Zack and questioning himself about why he is there. He knows every kid in the gym and had even been friends with some of them back in the sixth grade, which was several tattoos and piercings ago. He's self-conscious about not fitting in with the jocks and cheerleader types, and now he's on their turf.

Joel's senses are maxed. He is uncomfortable . . . on many levels.

————————————

Zack hopes that the peace he feels has a calming effect on Joel, like the way radiating heat from a fire helps warm those who are near the flames.

He notices that a few of his friends are giving them weird looks, and a couple make sneering comments that can be easily overheard. He wonders if some of those dirty looks are aimed at him for sitting with Joel. If this were yesterday and Joel showed up at the match, then Zack may have been one of the kids gawking at Joel. But not today.

In fact, Zack is seeing the world from Joel's perspective. It had to be hard to be dissed 24/7.

Kelly is playing well, and her kill shot takes the first set, 25-18. It's time to go.

"Dude, I have to watch Ty and Emma, so let's get out of here, okay?" Zack says. "We can hang out at my house."

Joel immediately comes to his feet during the time-out between sets. Looking to Zack, he replies, "Uh, whatever."

As the two exit the gym, Zack's early morning dream is popping back into his thoughts again. This time he's not freaking out about it. He welcomes the feelings, embraces the memories. He sees how the fans cheering him on were making him feel bigger and better, that they somehow lifted his confidence. He is also aware that in this real-life "game," prayer and support from others are just like the crowd—guiding him and helping him in a way that makes him better.

Zack understands that Joel will need someone to trust before he will be ready to talk about the stuff going on in his life. Zack also understands that anyone who could imagine catastrophic destruction needs some serious help.

More help than Zack can offer by himself.

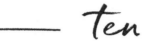

ten

INSIDE THE TOWERS' home, Joel follows Zack into his bedroom, taking in the posters of baseball's top hitters like his hometown favorite, Mike Trout.

"You can sit here," Zack says, pointing to one of the twin beds. Zack makes small talk about the Angels' chances to make the playoffs, but Joel knows what he really wants to talk about—the fantasized payback.

Sure enough, Zack segues into the topic and describes a Viking-like angel and everything they saw—explosions at the lockers, a madhouse of chaos in the hallway, the screams of the injured, and the carnage of the dead.

Once again, Joel is stunned. *Crazy . . . this is exactly what I envisioned in my mind just the other day.*

Layers of hurt, bitterness, confusion, and resentment had built up around Joel's heart over the last couple of years, but in Zack's room, like an onion, one layer at a time peels off.

There are still many, many layers to go.

———

Zack folds his arms after giving Joel the lowdown on the incredible experience he had with Ashkah and witnessing the bombing attack at North Valley High. When there's a pause in their conversation, Zack prays silently, seeking guidance.

What do I do now, Lord? Can You let me know how I can help?

Zack knows that he was in the right place at the right time, but he also knows that he is definitely in over his head.

Love him.

Is that Ashkah's voice? His dad's echo? His own thoughts? Or is it God's still small voice whispering in his heart? Zack isn't sure, but suddenly he knows what to do.

"Joel," Zack begins, "that was some deep stuff I approached you about during lunch. Seriously. You have my word that I won't tell the other kids about it, but you need to talk to someone who can help you with all the stuff going on. The pain. The issues. You know what I mean?" Zack pauses, then says, "Anyone come to mind . . . like maybe someone you trust?"

Joel lowers his head and speaks in a monotone.

"Zack, if you told me this morning that I would be sitting in your bedroom talking to you like this, I never would have believed it. But, man, let me think . . . ."

Joel leans back, reflecting—almost relaxing as he searches for an answer. "This feels crazy to say, but my dad's brother is someone who has tried to be there for me. I think my Uncle Chuck would talk with me. You know, he's reached out to me a couple times. I think he gets me. But I always pushed him away. It's like I was comfortable in my pain. Like I knew that I was right and the world was wrong. But dude, what's so weird is that I was totally locked into this."

"I know what you mean," Zack says. "And I bet your Uncle Chuck would be stoked to help you get on a better path. Don't you think?"

"Yeah, you could be right. Maybe . . . maybe I could reach out to him."

"You should. You won't regret talking to somebody."

Zack utters another nearly silent prayer: *Lord, if Joel talks to his Uncle Chuck, give his uncle the wisdom he needs.*

Zack's mind shifts back to the mayhem that Ashkah showed him earlier that day.

"Hey, Joel . . . umm, I got a question for you." Zack takes a deep breath to steady himself. "Do you actually have the stuff you thought about? You know, the explosives and gun and . . . well, you know, all that stuff?"

Joel lets Zack's question linger for a moment as he absorbs the seriousness of it all. "Zack, it freaks me out that I played all that out in my head. I was so lost in my anger and darkness that it felt like it was 'okay' to even imagine all that. Man, totally crazy . . . but did I buy all that stuff? Heck no."

Zack exhales and some tension dissipates. "Whew, Joel. I'm totally glad to hear that."

Zack notices Joel starting to get his things together. "Hey, you're welcome to hang out longer. My mom baked some killer chocolate chip cookies yesterday, and we have plenty left over."

"Thanks, but I'd better be getting along. It's a trip, but I'm glad you invited me over. You know, this has been one weird day."

Zack smiles back, nodding his head in the affirmative. "Hundred percent!" he replies.

As Joel is leaving Zack's room, he stops at the doorway. His left foot is in the hallway, and his right foot is still in Zack's room. It's like he isn't ready to leave. Not yet.

Wait a minute. Is that Ashkah gently nudging Joel back into his room?

"Hey, is it alright if I hang out a little longer?"

"Yeah, sure. Of course. Whatever you want."

As Zack nods, he looks past Joel. His eyes fix on Ashkah, who's kneeling in prayer in the hallway.

Joel doesn't say anything. He's contemplating, and then a video plays in his mind.

He sees himself in the sixth grade going through an awkward stage. His body is physically changing. He's maturing ahead of most of his classmates. His voice is changing and cracking. He has more than just some peach fuzz on his face, but his parents aren't paying much attention and provide zero guidance during his awkward transition into puberty.

Then in seventh grade, he gets zits—a ton of them. This time his parents do notice and take him to a dermatologist, which is so embarrassing. There is so much confusion and insecurity in junior high: the carefree days of surfing after school in sixth grade are long gone. Except for the trips to the dermatologist's office, his parents are not there for him. They had never been a close-knit family, but now they have a kid with a face full of zits, and they emotionally abandon him.

Life's pretty crummy. He's untouched by his parents, unaccepted by his peers, unsure in life, over-thinking everything, bitter, angry, in near isolation, anxious, depressed, and alone. Very alone.

But one crew doesn't totally shun him when he hits high school—the freaks, the outcasts on campus. They aren't the loving type, but at least they don't bother him. They don't laugh at him or recoil when he is nearby. They understand the need for someone to be accepted or left alone, but at least not ridiculed for being different. Joel likes that. And he likes that they hate the same people who blow him off.

But Joel can't let go of the bitterness he feels toward those that aren't there for him when he needs them. His bitterness goes unchecked and takes on a life of its own. He sees himself as a victim. He rationalizes his hate for others and buries his emotions under more layers of hate. Each layer of his dark clothing, intimidating tattoos, and piercings represent a layer of hate covering the real Joel.

What Joel can't see at this moment is Ashkah on his knees, praying that he will have his eyes and heart re-opened and realize that God knows everything happening to him . . . and that he is fully accepted and loved by Him.

Joel breaks away from the healing session and memories, then nods in the direction of Zack.

"Alright, Zack, I just had some stuff I was still thinking about. Man, this has been a lot to process, but I guess I'm all set," he says. "I'm heading out."

———————

Anyone other than Zack would have wondered why Joel just stood halfway in the hallway and halfway in his room, silently gazing off in his own world. But Zack figures that inner healing is beginning to take root and knows that Ashkah's prayers are warming Joel's heart. It's a powerful and soothing experience.

"Hey, tomorrow morning, bright and early at 6 a.m. at The Point, right?" Zack asks.

Joel pauses before answering. "Sure."

Zack is stoked, just the answer he was hoping for.

ABOUT A HALF hour after Joel leaves the Towers' house, Maggie steps into the house from the driveway.

"Can anyone help me set the table?" Maggie shouts out as she sets her light coat in the closet next to the front door.

Zack usually pretends he doesn't hear requests like that, but today's a new day. He leaves his bedroom, greets his mom, and helps her set the dining room table for five people.

Maggie knows how to create a great meal for hungry kids. In no time at all, she whips up her own version of bean quesadillas by filling soft flour tortillas with black beans, cheddar cheese, a diced-up onion, and a few spices. Then, one by one, she places them on two skillets set on the gas cooktop.

Peter arrives home as she's flipping over the quesadillas, which are browned on one side. "Mexican again?" he asks after giving her a quick kiss on the lips. "I thought after lunch at Eduardo's that you'd—"

Maggie places both hands on her hips and whispers, "Listen, we both know I don't like Mexican food as much as you do, but the kids sure love it."

With that, Maggie starts cutting an avocado to make guacamole and dices up two tomatoes into bits, which she sets on the table with a bowl of chips. Out of nowhere, Tyler and Emma come out of their bedrooms to munch.

With all five Towers in the kitchen, everyone sits down as Maggie sets a plate of folded-over bean quesadillas in the center of the dining table.

"Yummy, Mommy!" Emma says.

"Thank you, dear. Peter, you want to say the blessing?" Maggie asks.

"Sure," her husband replies. Reaching out his hands, the family falls in line and grasps hands with each other.

"Lord, thank you for this family," Peter prays, "and thank you for this meal. We ask that You bless this food to our bodies and use each of us to bring glory to You and Your kingdom. Amen."

Maggie and the children echo the "amen" one by

one as they simultaneously reach for the plate of warm quesadillas.

"Hey, kids. Don't worry. There are plenty, and your mother can fix more," Peter says before turning to his daughter on his right. "So Emmer, how was your day? Did you get to bless anyone?"

Emma beams. "Well, it went like this. Vickie was kinda upset about not having the right type of pencil for our test, so I gave her one of mine," she replied.

"That's great!" Maggie says, reaching across the table to make a high five with Emma.

"I'm not done," Emma jumps back in. "Then Vickie and I were at the swings during lunch, and she was all upset about her parents. Said that they were talking about getting a divorce."

"Greg and Sue?" Maggie shoots a concerned look at Peter. She is rattled. Greg and Sue are good friends of theirs, but they had no inkling about this news.

"Yup," Emma continues, "so I told her how you are always telling us to pray about stuff. So guess what?"

"What?" says Peter. "I can't wait to hear this."

"Right there on the swings, I asked if I could pray for her, and she said yes. I asked God to help her parents stop fighting and to help them get along better. And then I said the amen." Emma put an emphasis on the *I*.

"Wow!" Peter says with a proud look. "Now that's a great example of blessing someone. You know, Em, that's what I'm talking about. Maybe your brothers could learn a little something from you."

Peter's eyes lock in on Zack, then Tyler, with a look that says, *Hope you're learning a lesson here.*

"You know, I kinda had a blessing experience too," Tyler blurts out.

"Tell us," Maggie says as she spreads guacamole over her quesadilla.

"I was meeting the guys at lunch. We were eating inside today, and I see this kid. His name is Harold, and he was by himself. So, I remember what you said about blessing someone who needs a friend . . ."

"Exactly," Peter jumps in. "When you reach out—"

Tyler regains control of the conversation with a slight moan and eyes rolling. "Dad, I get it. So, anyway, this guy, Harold was all alone, or at least he didn't look like he had anyone to sit with at lunch today. So I had him join me and Bill and Mike and Fluff—you know, the guys. So check this out. He sits with us, and my friends are looking at me like I'd just lost it, right? But it turns out that this kid wasn't so bad after all. Sounds like he really knows how to play the guitar."

"That's great to hear, Ty," Maggie says, happy that some of their parenting is sticking. "Good job."

"Yeah, so Harold is going to give some lessons to four of us next week. He really isn't that bad of a guy. When I saw him after school, he was all smiles, and I think it was because I had him join us for lunch."

"That's awesome, son," Peter says, his chest swelling with pride. "What a day for the Towers kids! Those are two of the best things you two could have done today. If you brought home straight A's, I wouldn't be prouder. Well done!"

"Hey, pass the watermelon," Zack asks Emma, who was on her second helping.

"What about you, Zack?" Maggie asks. "You know your dad, and I had you on our hearts today. We prayed for you about whatever challenges you were facing."

Zack's stops chewing. Then he resumes. Maggie is wondering what was going on with Zack that led her—no, compelled her—to pray as she did throughout the day.

"Oh, it was a crazy day," Zack says with a subtle smile and slight head shake that matches his total exhaustion. After an exhale, he adds, "But I did get a chance to talk to Joel today."

"Talk to Joel?" Tyler interjects. "Zack had him over here at the house after school."

Maggie tries not to register any surprise, but now she's curious. *Zack spoke to that troubled kid—and brought him over to the house after school?*

Peter, though, can barely contain himself. "Really? That's amazing. I'm proud of you. So tell us what happened?"

"I'm so spent. How about I tell you and Mom about it later. Okay?"

"Sure, son," Peter says.

———

Toward 9 p.m., after his brother and sister are already in bed, Zack leaves his bedroom and finds his parents watching cable news and getting caught up on the events of the day.

Peter glances at the Weather app on his phone. "Looks like Santa Ana winds are coming in," he says, referring to the hot winds that come off the California desert and boost temperatures into the 90s and triple digits.

"Yeah, the offshore breeze might be really good for the surf," Zack says. "I told Joel that I'd go out to The Point with him before school tomorrow."

"That's really nice of you," Maggie says. "So tell us why you had Joel over to the house."

Zack runs a hand through his brown hair. "Yeah, about that. Something totally weird happened today. I wasn't sure how to talk about this at dinner. I'm still processing a lot, and I'm not even sure how to tell you guys. You know, I'm not sure you're going to believe it."

"Try us," Peter says.

"Okay."

Zack proceeds to lay out the entire story—eating lunch in the Quad, the turkey and Swiss sandwich, the arrival of Ashkah, walking the hallways, the horrific bombings . . . the entirety of the experience. He doesn't hold anything back.

His parents are cold-stone statues. They don't say anything. Zack wonders if they think he's crazy, but he's not getting a judging vibe at all. They are just stunned.

When he's done, after a moment to process and breath, his father speaks first. "Wow, Zack. Your mother and I had an inkling something was going to happen today. We even met for lunch just to pray for you. But holy cow . . . we didn't realize all that was going on!"

Maggie looks over at Peter and can tell that he's still getting his head around what he just heard.

"That is just amazing," he says.

Her head is spinning too as she wraps her mind around the magnitude of everything that happened.

After another long pause, Maggie catches her breath and chimes in, "Zack, I'm amazed that you were invited by the Lord to be a part of such a powerful vision. You know, the Bible tells us that 'Young men will see visions.' I'm sure that is what happened to you."

As if seamlessly continuing in the same flow, Peter continues, "I mean, most people will live a long life and never experience anything like that. It sure sounds like the Lord sent an angel to show you a vision and to protect you and invite you into His work to reach Joel."

"I was thinking the same thing," Maggie adds. "When Dad and I met for lunch today, we prayed for you. I really had a sense that you were facing a difficult situation. Then just after lunch, Dad and I both felt that you were okay somehow, and that whatever it was, maybe you were getting past the challenge."

Maggie is smiling, taking in the moment, and feeling the peace of the Lord. She moves over to hug Zack and lets her motherly love communicate warmth and safety as only a mother's hug can.

After a few more minutes of silence, not an awkward silence but rather a peaceful, comfortable moment, Zack starts up.

"Crazy that you guys were praying for me right when Ashkah visited me. Well, I do feel like God is more real than I ever imaged. You know, more tangible today. I'm not sure that I fully grasp all that is going on, but one thing's for sure . . . it's got me thinking. Thinking differently. Like there is a lot more to life, and a lot going on with other people."

With a long exhale, he continues, "It's been an exhausting day, a lot to take in. And I can't believe that I still have some homework to finish before I can get some sleep."

His parents nod in agreement and approach him for a long group hug. The three of them huddle together for thirty seconds, silent and soaking it all in. All that can be heard are long deep breaths.

Peter starts in with a prayer of thanksgiving, acknowledging God's greatness and His love. "We ask that each of us will be open to all that You are teaching us, especially Zack. We pray this in Your holy name."

The trio each utter an amen but stay in the silence that follows for a few moments more.

Maggie gently breaks the silence. "Honey, we love you." And then she offers one more hug.

———

There isn't much that needs to be said in that moment, but Zack knows that just as a butterfly can never be a caterpillar again, he will never be the same after today . . . in a good way.

And that brings a smile to his tired face.

Tuesday

— twelve —

WITH TOTAL FOCUS, Zack's bat continues to accelerate. The impact point is perfect, right on the fat of
the bat. The ball that decelerated just prior to reaching
home plate is now accelerating at an unfathomable rate.

The crowd rises to its feet as the struck ball lifts
and soars. Zack's eyes are still locked on the point of
contact; he has not yet raised his head to track the ball
that launched off his bat. His entire body uncoils like
a spring, from the feet up through hips, ending with a
turn of his shoulders. At that moment, he knows he hit
the ball hard enough to land in the upper deck beyond

the left-center field wall.

What Zack doesn't know is if the fly ball has the combination of height and distance to clear the fence. As he drops his bat and gains his balance, he starts his sprint toward first base. Until the first base coach delivers the signal that the ball has cleared the fence, he will run all out.

With adrenaline pumping, Zack focuses on taking a wide path to round first base so that he can have a proper angle to go on to second base. The first base coach is frantically making windmill motions to keep running—

That means at least two runners will score. Will the man on first also come around to score and tie up the game? Or did he hit it out of the park for a Game 7 walk-off grand slam that won the World Series?

The loud explosion of sound assaults Zack's ears. The hometown fans are cheering thunderously as the base runners advance. Zack knows that he's going to round first. He's digging in for two—

"Watch out for the remnants of a two-car collision on the 405 North at Harbor that has early morning traffic backed up to Fairview."

Seriously? Not again, Zack thinks. Almost the perfect dream again. He taps his phone app to turn off his alarm and rubs his eyes.

What time is it?

He glances at his phone again. The time at the top of his screen says 5:40. Why an hour-and-a-half early? Then he remembers. He said he was going to meet Joel at The Point for a surf session before school.

Zack knows there's no time to lose. He gets up, throws on some board shorts and a hoodie sweatshirt, splashes some water on his face, and heads off to the garage. He'd loaded his surfboard on his bike's side rack the night before. He's always liked the shortened nose and wider tail on his board.

He and his family live about a mile from the beach, but their neighborhood is on a foothill, so the ride is generally all downhill. The cool morning air is brisk but not cold.

Joel is waiting for him when he arrives at 6:03. The first rays of orange sunlight light up the eastern sky. It's a glorious morning, and the water is glassy. Zack's happy that the surf is small—under three feet—considering he hasn't surfed since school started up in the fall.

Zack can tell how good Joel is just by the way he paddles out. His arms work in unison, and Zack mimics him and gets into the flow. Once they reach the lineup, they sit on their boards. The water is chilly; about half the guys are wearing wetsuits. Joel has his wetsuit on. Zack makes a mental note to bring his next time.

Zack notices that Joel is pretty aggressive about picking up waves. Unlike at the gym yesterday, today Joel is in his element. Just then, a nice wave comes his way. Not too big. Zack is in the perfect spot. Two quick paddles, and he drops in, makes a bottom turn, and works the wave as he rides the shoulder. Like riding a bike. A bit rough, but you never forget.

The surf session isn't solely about catching waves. Between sets, he and Joel sit on their boards next to each other, but they don't do a lot of talking. When they do talk, it's not about serious stuff. The session is more about enjoying the water and the beauty of the early morning vibe.

After about forty minutes, Zack looks at his water-proof watch and then at Joel. "I think we have to go in," Zack says.

"You were always the type never to miss first period." Joel replies with a slight smirk on his face.

Zack laughs. "Blame my parents. Besides they'd kill me if I didn't go to class."

They paddle in and load their boards on their bikes. With a "See you later," Zack takes off, but riding home takes longer since it's mostly uphill. With each pedal stroke, he thinks about how much his life has changed in the last twenty-four hours.

At home, Maggie is getting breakfast ready for the family while Peter sips on his Nespresso coffee and scrolls through his iPad. She hears Zack blast into the house from the garage. When he passes by the kitchen, he's sopping wet.

"Gotta shower," he says as he sprints by.

"Thanks for coming home on time." Maggie notices her son taking the stairs two at a time up to his bedroom on the second floor.

Peter looks up and grunts. He has the app for his local newspaper open on his tablet and is scrolling through an article about teenage drug use.

"Hey, Maggie. Did you read this article about rampant

substance abuse among teens?"

"I saw the link but didn't have time to click on it. But it looks like we need to sit down with the boys again."

Unlike Peter, Maggie never so much as tried a cigarette. As a youth, she was never tempted to experiment with drugs. She knew friends in school who couldn't resist trying drugs and really messed up their lives.

Maggie continues toasting bagels and slicing up apples. She is setting everything on plates when Zack bounds down the stairs, his wet hair slicked back and his clothes a bit wet.

"Well, looks like you showered in record time," she says. "Tyler and Emma aren't even down yet."

"That's because I'm hungry," Zack says.

"Well, you probably burned a lot of calories out there in the water," Maggie replies. "I have toasted bagels and sliced apples. Or you can choose a cereal," she remarks.

"Cheerios will be fine."

Maggie watches her son reach for the box of Honey Nut Cheerios and pour nearly a full bowl. *He is a creature of habit.*

Peter looks up. "Zack, I'm reading this interesting article about teen drug use. What's it like on campus? Is there a lot of drug use going on?"

"Dad, you can be so lame sometimes. You know that my friends are not doing that kind of stuff."

Maggie shoots Peter a quick look. She has a mother's sense that Zack is not being as transparent as he could be.

"Well, let's talk tonight," Maggie suggests.

"Okay, we can do that. But check this out: I had a

pretty cool surf session with Joel today."

She knows when her son is changing the topic. She can go with the flow.

"What?" she asks.

"Joel and I kind of connected this morning in the water. We didn't say much, but there was a comfortable vibe. Not too weird. It's not like we're buds now, but it was cool."

Peter looks up from his iPad again. With his attention fully on Zack, he says, "That's great to hear, son. You're really making a difference!"

"Morning, Mom. Hi, Dad." Emma, with her curly hair combed, takes a seat at the kitchen table and reaches for one of the toasted bagels.

"I'm here, too." It's Tyler. He prefers Wheaties over Cheerios and pours himself a big bowl.

"Hey guys, we've got about ten minutes before this bus leaves. Make sure that you have your stuff ready," Peter says.

Tyler stifles a groan. "Got it, Dad."

"And kids, remember: make good choices today," Maggie instructs. She's serious, but she makes sure she tempers her words with a smile. She senses that she needs to impart this advice with a little more energy this morning.

The kids finish breakfast quickly and get their backpacks ready.

"I'll get the dishes," she says as she starts cleaning up. She stops to kiss each of her children on the cheek. That's important for her.

Her last kiss is for her husband.

"I'll call you later," Peter says. "Love you."

As the kids pile into the SUV, Peter feels like he is still glowing from the impact his kids made yesterday and the spiritual growth taking place in Zack's heart.

Their neighbor Justin is waiting out front on the sidewalk. He takes his usual seat in the rear bench next to Zack. "Okay Emmer, you're first up. I'm stoked about what you did yesterday." Peter's smile gets brighter as he thinks about how Emma reached out to Vickie.

Within a few minutes, he swings into the drop-off zone at Meyer Street Elementary. "There you go, Sweetie. Have a great day, and remember to bless someone. Find someone to be nice to today."

"Okay, Dad. Love you. And thanks." Emma runs off with her oversized Hurley backpack bouncing against her back with each step.

Vernon Junior High is their next stop.

"Ty, looks like you are getting it, buddy. You did a great thing with Harold. Keep up the good work. Find someone to bless today."

"Thanks, Dad. I will."

Tyler hops out from the front passenger seat and spots a couple of friends. Before leaving, he turns back and waves to his dad, his brother, and Justin.

"There's a good kid," Peter says to the two boys in the back. "All right. Next stop, NV."

Peter looks in his rearview mirror at Justin sitting next to Zack in the far back.

"Hey, Justin. You ever see someone at school that looks like they could use a smile?"

Justin wants to disappear. He turns to Zack for support, but Zack doesn't say anything.

"Um, Mr. Towers. I guess so," Justin quietly answers.

"Well, you ought to offer a smile to that person today."

Peter wants to laugh, seeing how uncomfortable and embarrassed Justin is, but he keeps a straight face in hopes that Justin will follow through.

Zack, however, is cracking up and obviously enjoying Justin's discomfort.

Peter notices. "Take it easy on Justin," he says with a smile on his face. "But hey, love what you are doing, Zack. Great job with Joel. It will be cool to see how he responds."

"I know what you mean," Zack replies, as he is eager to see Joel and check in.

Peter glances directly at Zack, "Yep, and remember to stay alert for Joel and others who may be in need of your help."

As the SUV pulls up to one of the drop-off areas at North Valley High, Peter has one last thing to say to the both of them. "You've been blessed, so remember to be a blessing to someone."

"I'll try," Justin says. "Thanks for the ride." He keeps his head down and avoids eye contact.

"Hey, Dad, thanks for the ride, and remember to bless someone today too," Zack teases.

Peter grins. *That kid has his mother's sense of humor.*

— thirteen —

As Emma puts her things away in her "locker," which is more like a cubbyhole that each kid in Mrs. Cranston's class is assigned to store their backpacks, jackets, and lunches, she catches up with Vickie.

"Hey, Vickie, how's it going?"

"Well, we had one night with my parents not yelling, so who knows? Maybe that prayer worked." Vickie is almost smiling and definitely not depressed like she was the day before.

The two of them make their way to the side-by-side desk they share.

With Emma on the right side, they take their spots and continue to talk about boys, Mrs. Cranston's not-too-cool outfit, if the girls would be nice to Meagan today, what they would eat for lunch . . . the usual topics.

It's another normal day at school.

Tyler meets up with Mike in front of the gym on their way to the main building. They make their way to the hallway that will take them to Mrs. Goldman's homeroom.

Tyler looks up and sees Harold coming in his direction. Just before they pass each other, Tyler lets out a friendly, "Wassup, bud!"

"Hey, Tyler. Good, thanks," Harold replies with a nervousness that is amplified by having responded with "Good, thanks" instead of the more appropriate, "Not much."

Tyler isn't fazed by the misspeak and actually thinks Harold looks a bit more relaxed than he did yesterday. As they leave Harold behind, they continue on their way to their homeroom.

"Dude, he's such a wannabe," Mike says to Tyler. "Such a loser."

"Cut him some slack. He's a good guy, and he'll figure it out soon enough. Besides, what do you care? You're getting some free guitar lessons. I betcha he's pretty good."

"We'll find out," Mike replies with a hint of skepticism.

Zack and Justin go in opposite directions to get to class. Zack is in the hallway just outside of his first period classroom when Kelly finds him.

Seeing her reminds Zack how great he feels since yesterday's bizarre experience. The alternate reality portrayed such tragedy, but real life had miraculously yielded a positive outcome. Here he stands, face to face with Kelly, who he really likes.

"So, did you go to The Point with Joel before school?" she asks.

"Yeah, it was great. I mean I only caught one wave that's worth talking about, but Joel hasn't forgotten how to surf. He can really shred."

"Is that what I was supposed to be praying about?"

"Part of it. I'm really wanting to reach out to him and see him get his life back. You know, to be normal agai . . ."

Zack catches himself and realizes that his words are sounding too judgmental. "I mean, you know, to be happy again," he says.

"I think that what you're doing is really nice, Zack Towers."

Zack likes hearing her say his full name. Then she surprises him by leaning in and giving him a kiss on the cheek.

"See you at lunch, Brother Teresa."

"Aren't you being funny."

"I can be when I want to be."

With that, Kelly is off to class.

———

When Peter arrives at work, he notices a flashing inter-office email message awaiting him. He has been a partner at Skyles, Towers & Abbott for five years, and their media agency is growing faster than anyone anticipated.

Peter is the creative force behind the agency, and the message is letting him know that he will be managing a new account.

About a year ago, Peter had pitched the local police department about launching a new anti-drug D.A.R.E. campaign. The police department wants to know if a new, updated campaign would be relevant to kids, so they're looking at his media agency to run a full-blown test.

Skyles, Towers & Abbott offered to do the job at cost. Peter remembers arguing that the project should be about helping the community, not about adding to their bottom line.

Peter is delighted when he reads the e-mail and learns that he will, as requested, lead the job.

Wow, he thinks. *Here I am, ready to talk to my kids about drugs, and this project literally lands on my lap.*

He knows that to do this project right, he will have to meet with the police department's anti-drug personnel to find out about their current program and why they want to make a change. He needs to understand their goals and how they will measure and define success.

In order to make a good start, Peter is eager to research the latest data about drug use for teenagers. Is the opioid epidemic reaching down into the junior high grades? And how about abuse and misuse of other prescription drugs?"

"Thank you, Lord, for bringing this project to me," he whispers.

———

Maggie is getting ready to meet some of the ladies at Café Angelicas. This is a new chic place in town that offers healthy salads, hearty soups, and artisan sandwiches. The trendy café fits in perfect with the Southern California foodie scene.

Maggie, Sandra, and Sue arrive first. They take an outside table while they wait for the other three to join them.

"Sue, how's everything going?" Maggie doesn't want to overtly pry in front of Sandra, but since it was just the three of them . . .

"So-so." Sue's Korean accent is slight but noticeably pronounced. She is in her mid-thirties, could easily pass for her late twenties, and is athletic and trim, not soft around the middle like many moms.

"So-so? What's going on? Is everything okay?" Maggie asks tenderly.

Sue sighs. Maggie can tell that she is weighing whether she could open up to her and Sandra.

"Greg and I have had some issues, but last night things started going in the right direction. At this point, who knows what's going to happen between us?" Sue looks at Maggie with a slight glint of hope in her eyes.

"Wow, I didn't know things had been so stressed." Maggie does not want to let on what she heard from Emma.

"Really? Well, Vickie told me about the prayer on the swings with your daughter." Sue cannot hold back a little chuckle.

"Okay . . . I wasn't sure that I was supposed to know anything," Maggie replies with a friendly smile.

"What are you guys talking about?" Sandra interjects.

Maggie continues looking at Sue. "Yeah, I did hear something from Emma, but Peter and I had no idea . . . and we weren't sure what to make of Emma's encounter."

"Someone has got to fill me in," Sandra says.

"Okay, but real quick, before the others arrive," Sue says.

———

During lunch period at North Valley, Kelly and Zack are joined in the Quad by Corey, Andy, Lauren, and Julie. After a couple of minutes of the typical lunch time banter, Zack looks around the Quad. He spots Joel at his usual spot—the rock. He's alone.

As if Joel knows that Zack would be looking for him, Joel looks in Zack's direction.

Earlier that morning, while in the lineup, Joel told Zack that he could not imagine ever eating with anyone else in the Quad. Zack figures that Joel finds it more comfortable . . . safer . . . to chill at his spot.

Joel smiles and nods to Zack, who returns the smile. At that moment, Zack realizes that Joel didn't use any black eyeliner today. Instead of two solid black T-shirts layered with black jeans, Joel is wearing one black shirt. A minor change, but Zack notices.

Zack believes that there is a young man with a wealth of potential just below the layers of black. Just like the layers of paint at the junior high that cover the image of the old mascot—a formidable, strong tiger.

Joel is a young man, made in the image of his creator, but he's been buried beneath layers. Layers of hate, hurt, and isolation. Today, a layer has been removed.

Zack rejoins the conversation at his table, and, as usual, tries to steal some of Kelly's lunch. Kelly predictably acts as if it's a big deal to let Zack have half her sandwich, but as they both know, it really isn't.

Just as lunch is wrapping up, Zack is pretty sure that he overhears Lauren invite Andy over to Brett's place after school.

Pay attention, you are needed. You can make a difference.

Oh no, not again. Zack looks around to make sure that Ashkah isn't behind him. Whew, he's alone . . . except for seventy-five other kids in the Quad.

Pay attention, be alert. They need to be loved.

"See you after school, Zack?"

"Yeah, sure, Kelly. See you later."

Zack is smiling on the outside for Kelly, but on the inside he is still pondering the gentle instructions he just heard. It sure sounded like Ashkah, or was it from Zack's heart?

Or perhaps it was the echo of his dad's encouragement from earlier that morning?

He isn't sure, but he has a feeling that he is about to find out.

fourteen

PETER IS BUSY at the agency working on the D.A.R.E. campaign. The modern conference room, outfitted with an oversized conference table that sits twenty, is occupied by Peter, a project manager, and three police officers tasked as liaisons. The table is strewn with various renderings of campaign layouts.

One side of the conference room has floor-to-ceiling windows with epic views of the eastern foothills. The other side is waist-high-to-ceiling frosted glass that blurs details of the people passing by in the hallway or the cubicles outside the conference room.

That morning Peter learns about drug, alcohol, and

tobacco use among children. It is a sobering update. Students and their parents need this education campaign.

After school, Zack walks Kelly home and then continues alone to his house.

Zack is lost in his thoughts. "Who's in need? Love who?" he half-prays and half-asks out loud.

He is not ready or in the mood to be whisked into the future by his large, angelic friend. He is fatigued from yesterday and the early morning surf session at daybreak. At the same time, he is unsure about exactly what he heard in his heart.

As Zack gets within a half of a block of his house, his dream bursts back into his mind like a firecracker. He sees the first base coach waving his arm in a windmill motion, willing him to run like his life depends upon it. Zack is digging deep to make the turn at first base and clearly remembers his cleats striking the inner corner of the bag as sets his attention to second base.

"What are you doing home so early?" his mother asks. Maggie just happened to be standing at the front door as Zack strolls up the walkway. She has the day's mail in her hand.

He was so deep in reflection, pondering the dream, that his mom's comments jolted him back to reality sooner than expected. Her voice is gentle, but no matter—it startles him. He flutters like the SUV, but this time the moment passes in seconds.

Adjusting to the real world, like the transition he makes when his alarm goes off in the morning, he regains his footing. After a deep breath and repeating the question to himself, just to make sure he is tracking, he answers his mom.

"Practice was canceled, and Kelly had no match, so I thought I'd come right home. Besides, I'm tired from surfing this morning. I guess I'm not used to getting up that early."

"Well, that was a nice thing you did. I'm sure you were a real blessing to Joel."

As the family gathers for dinner, Maggie looks forward to one of her favorite times of the day. Hanging with the kids and hearing them talk about what happened at school is always a rich experience for her.

"Vickie was happier today," Emma starts without prompting. "She wasn't so depressed and was like normal. We did each other's hair and talked about stuff."

Maggie doesn't think Emma's hair looks any different than when she left in the morning, but she isn't going to say anything. She figures "doing each other's hair" just meant that they brushed it.

"That's great," Maggie chimes in. "When I met up with Vicki's mom today, she shared that her and Greg are working on their marriage. She sounded concerned but was also a little bit optimistic."

Maggie puts a subtle emphasis on "a little bit" as she shoots a quick look at Peter as if to say, *Let's keep praying for them.*

"Well, Ty, what about you?" Peter asks. "Anything to share?"

Tyler nods and flashes a smile that reveals a bit of salad stuck to his teeth. Maggie, ever the mom, gestures to Tyler to do something about the piece of romaine lettuce stuck between his top front teeth.

"Yeah, today was pretty cool," Tyler begins. "I was with Mike when we ran into Harold. I think he's coming out of his shell. I got all thinking that I must be pretty rad to be the kid reaching out to Harold and saying hi to him, but then at lunch I saw Fluff talking to Harold and stuff. So it's not just me talking to Harold. Then when I saw Harold at the end of the day, he was totally grinning again. It was cool."

"That's terrific!" Peter taps the dinner table with his right hand for emphasis. "I'm so glad you guys are getting this."

Then Peter turns to Zack. "How did our friend Justin do?"

"What?" Maggie asks, feeling the same way Sandra must have felt at lunch earlier in the day.

"Huh?" Tyler looks confused.

"Justin?" asks Emma.

———

Zack is glad that he didn't take a sip of milk before his dad asked that question. If he had, that would have resulted in 'milk dripping out of the nose' laughter. Still, he is grinning when he says, "Dad, that was so funny this morning."

Then, to the rest of the family, Zack continues. "Dad was giving his usual spiel about blessing somebody during the school day and Justin was just sitting there, minding his own business. Then Dad goes into his 'What about you, Justin? Is there someone you can bless?'"

Zack puts on his best imitation of his father's voice, but it sounds slow and deep—like an automated recording low on batteries.

"And no, Dad. I have no idea what Justin did today about the 'blessing' instruction."

When the chuckling dies down, Peter adds with a slight smile, "Well, we will just have to find out tomorrow."

When the Towers finish their kitchen clean up and each child begins to make their way toward their rooms for homework, Peter calls out to Zack. "Hey, Mom and I want to talk with you about something."

The three of them walk into the living room just off the open-concept kitchen. Peter and Maggie plant themselves on the couch, and Zack takes a seat on the over-sized ottoman facing his parents.

"What's up?"

Peter takes the lead. "We would like to talk to you about drugs. What's happening at North Valley? What are the common drugs and substances that are making their way to kids your age?"

Zack shrugs. "I told you guys already: there is no

big drug thing going on. Look, this isn't like your generation."

Zack chuckles a bit and adds, "We just aren't as into this stuff like you were when you were my age. This isn't the '80s."

"Zack, we're not looking to get anyone in trouble or for details about your friends and kids you know," Peter says. "I know that this can be awkward, but just try to fill us in a bit about what's going on. This will help me with my work for the D.A.R.E program."

Peter was still processing all the information he took in earlier in the day at the campaign kick-off meeting at work. At the same time, he is torn between seeking realistic insights about what type of drugs, vaping, and other substances are being used by kids Zack's age.

He is also curious—and concerned—whether Zack had experimented with any drugs. He realizes that he is too close to Zack to be truly objective.

———

Zack wonders where his father is going with this.

"Listen, there just isn't the amount of stuff going on that you think," he says, although being honest, he knows there are kids into that sort of thing.

Zack recalls times he steered away from certain friends because he knew they did some heavy drinking on weekends, vaped, or smoked some weed. Zack thinks he can't tell his parents about them because he isn't sure if his friends will get in trouble if he spills everything he knows.

"Well, just know this," Peter begins. "This drug stuff is really harmful. Like it can really jack with your body and mind. You know what I mean. Some of the drugs off the street contain all sorts of contaminated or harmful ingredients, and some drug combinations can be dangerous."

His mother adds, "We do not want you doing any drinking or smoking . . . of anything."

Zack can tell that his mother wants him to hear this message loud and clear because of her tone and body language.

He has to reassure her and his father. "I haven't forgot about your 'talks' in the past, and yes, I promise you that I haven't done any drinking or drugs." Actually, the part about not drinking isn't one hundred percent true since he drinks a few beers on occasion.

His father relaxes. "Okay, that's good to hear. I'm just concerned because I'm getting a lot of new info from the police department for the new D.A.R.E. campaign I'm heading up. Let's come back to this in a couple days and go over this some more. Sound like a plan?"

"Yeah, sure." Zack's slight smile lets his parents know that he does not expect to gain anything from a mini stay-off-drugs speech from Dad and Mom.

Later that evening, at about 9:45 p.m., the home's landline phone rings.

Zack, wiped out from a long day, is still finishing his homework on the kitchen table. He grabs the landline phone before the ringing can wake up Emma, figuring it was some type of telemarketing call since he doesn't recognize the phone number. But a sales call at a quarter to ten?

"Hello?"

"Hey, what's up?"

Zack recognizes the voice of Brett, one of his friends from school.

"I was wondering if I could talk to your dad," he says in a hushed monotone.

Now that is highly unusual. "Yeah, sure, he's here."

Then with a louder voice, Zack calls out to his father who is watching TV in the living room. "Hey, Dad. You got a call. It's Brett. He wants to talk to you."

Zack's announcement comes across like a blend between a statement and a question.

His father rises up from the couch and accepts the phone from Zack.

"What's going on Brett?" Peter asks.

"Mr. Towers, I need a favor. Can you pick me up? I'm at the police station."

As Peter listens to Brett explain why he is being held by the police, he's surprised that the teen doesn't sound embarrassed. From the way Brett speaks, his voice and tone convey that he's sorrier to have disturbed Mr. Towers on a school night.

There is only one answer Peter can give to Brett. "Of course. I'll be right there."

As Peter gathers his keys and wallet, Zack rushes over to ask what's going on.

"Well, Brett is at the police station and needs me to pick him up."

"What? What happened?" Zack has a nervous look.

"He was drinking and got picked up by the police," Peter briefly explains as he makes his way out the front door. Turning back to Zack, he says, "If you're up when I get back, I'll fill you in then. Okay?"

Zack sits back down at the kitchen table, but he's freaking out and can't focus on finishing his homework.

What the heck is going on? What happened to Brett?

He decides to wait up for his dad to return home so that he can get some answers. He moves his tired and spent body to the family room and falls into his favorite leather chair.

After a couple minutes in the comfortable piece of furniture, it takes too much effort to keep his eyes open.

fifteen

As Zack leans back in the oversized leather chair with his legs resting on the equally oversized ottoman, his dream sputters back to his memory: Why is he running so fast to get to first base? Didn't he hit the ball hard enough to go over the fence?

He hears the triumphant roar of the crowd, but he also sees the look on the first base coach's face—*Go. Go. Move as fast as you can!*

Peter arrives at the police station. Even with stopping at the one traffic light between his home and the police station, it only took eight minutes to get there.

At the reception desk, Peter introduces himself to the on-duty officer. A phone call is made, and then he is led down a hall to a room by a police officer who introduces himself as Officer Greg Gable.

They stop at the fourth door on the right. With a swish of keys, the door swings open. Brett is sitting behind a table. Upon seeing Peter, the teen nearly jumps out of his chair.

"You okay?" Peter asks.

"Yes, Mr. Towers." Brett seems relieved that he can finally go home.

"So, please tell me what happened," Peter says to Officer Gable.

"Well, it wasn't pretty. You see, Brett was with three others, and they obtained hard liquor and were congregating at Lacey Park. My partner and I received a dispatch call. When we arrived, we approached the four of them and were able to confirm that they were inebriated. After standard protocols, we brought them in to the station. The two girls were released to their parents approximately one hour ago, and the other boy involved in this incident had more to drink than his body could handle. He collapsed in front of me, so our EMTs stepped in and shortly thereafter, the young man was rapidly dispatched to the hospital. This one"—pointing at Brett—"was not able to contact his parents, so when I asked him if he knew another adult in the area who could be responsible for him, someone I could release him to, he provided your name. So that's why you're here."

"Thank you, Officer Gable." And then to Brett, Peter asks, "Where are your parents?"

"They're out to dinner and a show in downtown L.A., so I couldn't reach them."

"Mr. Towers, if you are willing to sign this document, we will release Brett into your custody," Officer Gable says. He drops a folder on the table and opens up some paperwork for Peter to review.

"Absolutely."

As they leave the station, Peter decides to wait until they get in the car before asking Brett for his side of the story. Peter does not see a fifteen-year-old boy sitting next to him. Instead he sees the kid at eight, nine, ten, and eleven years old who he had coached in youth sports for many years.

To Peter's surprise, Brett has no problem talking openly about the night's drinking binge.

"Well, me and Andy had some tequila that we took from my dad's cabinet, then we met up with Lauren and Julie at the park. Andy drank the most. And I think he may have taken something else. But I'm not sure. He really drank a lot. I mean, he didn't seem to feel anything right away, so he kept right on drinking. Then Andy didn't look too good. He couldn't walk too straight either. We all thought that it was pretty funny until someone called the cops on us.

"Before we knew it, Officer Gable and another officer showed up in a cop car at about the same time Andy was looking really bad. Well, by the time we were taken to the police station, Andy threw up, which almost hit the policeman's shoes. Then Andy passed out. You already know that he was taken to the hospital. Then when I was the only one of us left at the police station, I called you. You know the rest, sir."

Peter knew he had to choose his words carefully. "Look, drinking is not as innocent and harmless as you may think. Every year I read about college kids going off to their freshman year with a mindset that alcohol is not dangerous. They think that they can drink all they want, and then they get caught up in these frat parties where there's tons of drinking games. Each year I read about kids who actually die from alcohol poisoning. Totally tragic. I know it sounds odd, but this is serious stuff."

Peter pauses to see if Brett is paying attention. *Yes, he is.*

As they drive up to Brett's house, Peter looks the young man in the eyes and says, "Okay, tell your folks what happened and ask your dad to call me tomorrow. Got that? And, be good."

"Yes, sir. I will. And, thank you, Mr. Towers, for picking me up."

"You're welcome Brett. Lots to learn from tonight."

Peter stays in the car, engine running, as he watches the fifteen-year-old walk away.

Brett turns to wave good-bye and respectfully nods his head toward Mr. Towers before disappearing behind the front door.

———

As Peter pulls into his driveway and makes his way to the front door, his mind struggles to find the right words for Zack. At the same time he's struck by how ironic it is that he and Maggie had started a conversation with Zack about drug use among school friends.

"Hey, Dad! What happened!" Zack shoots off the couch and greets his dad five steps inside the front door.

"Your friends Brett, Andy, Lauren, and Julie were out drinking at the park."

Peter checks Zack's expression to get a read on how he is taking the information. Zack, still wearing a nervous look, is slightly trembling. Peter interprets that to mean that Zack is concerned and paying close attention.

"They took a bottle of tequila from the liquor cabinet of Brett's dad, and Andy had a lot to drink. I'm not clear on the details, but he may have had something in addition to the alcohol. You see, sometimes the effect from alcohol can take a bit of time, and since Andy did not feel anything different, he just kept drinking."

Then Peter describes how Andy passed out but not before nearly puking all over the policeman's shoes.

"Is Andy okay?"

"No, son. He was taken by ambulance to Memorial Hospital."

"No way. I can't believe it." Zack takes a deep breath. Between yesterday and today, there's been a lot to process.

Peter thinks Zack is using his last bit of energy to process the news about Andy.

"Son, we have a lot to talk about, but it's getting

late and you've had a super long day. I love you, but let's talk in the morning." Peter puts his arm around his son's shoulders.

"Okay . . . goodnight. Love you, Dad."

Peter quietly makes his way to the master bedroom, hoping not to wake up Maggie. As he opens their bedroom door, he navigates his way around in the dark.

———

Maggie is suddenly fully awake but purposefully not moving an inch.

"Hey, babe. Why don't you turn the light on," she says from the bed.

"No, I don't want to totally wake you up. I can make it to the—"

Thump.

"Owee!"

"Find a piece of furniture?"

"Yeah. But I think my big toe will survive."

"So what happened out there tonight?"

Peter holds the big toe on his right foot with both hands for a few seconds, just enough time for the throbbing to settle down.

"Well, crazy timing considering my D.A.R.E. project."

For the next fifteen minutes, Maggie listens to her husband describe what happened at the police station with Brett and how Andy was rushed to the hospital.

As she listens, Maggie wonders how this might impact Zack . . . and if Andy will be okay.

"Dr. Edwin Hannaford. Paging Dr. Hannaford. Nurse's station."

The page rings out on the intercom system at Memorial Hospital.

Dr. Hannaford, wearing his white lab coat with an identification badge dangling from his left coat pocket, hustles to the nurse's station.

"Doctor, you're needed in 336 stat," says the nurse on duty.

He quickly enters into Room 336, Andy's room. The young boy looks listless as he lies in the bed with his eyes closed. A distraught woman, his mother, is at his side.

The nurse attending to Andy briefs the doctor about the boy's blood alcohol level, weakening vital signs, and possible organ damage.

"Thank you," Dr. Hannaford says to the nurse, but his eyes are already fixed on the boy.

Speaking in the direction of the woman at his bedside, he says, "You're the mother?"

"Yes, Doctor."

"How old is he?"

"Fifteen."

"Your son is in a coma. It looks like your son ingested considerable amounts of alcohol. Based on the blood tests, he also ingested alprazolam, commonly found in Xanax, which complicates things. We have a lot of work to do here."

Dr. Hannaford takes his eyes off Andy for the first time since entering the room and turns to Andy's mother.

"I'm sorry, but I have to ask you to leave the room. You can wait in the waiting area, and I will update you as soon as possible."

"Can't I stay? I still have questions, I really . . ."

Looking directly into her eyes, Dr. Hannaford interupts, "I'm afraid not. Sorry. But I will personally update you."

Then, with his focus turning back to Andy, the doctor gets to work as the shocked single-parent leaves the hospital room.

––––––

Andy's mom, Cathy Finch, finds her way to the waiting area and parks her tired, five-foot, four-inch frame in one of the padded armchairs. She pulls out her cell phone to make some calls to her closest friend, a neighbor, and her folks, but when she sees the time on her screen, she puts her phone back in her purse.

The calls will have to wait until first thing in the morning.

––––––

Zack is tossing and turning.

He is tired, very tired, but he is too anxious to sleep. He has to know how Andy is doing. Then Zack thinks about the crowd cheering him in his dream, the confidence that builds within him. The strength he receives from the crowd is like the empowerment he feels from his parent's prayers, from Ashkah, and from the Lord.

He rolls out of bed and kneels. "Please God, keep Andy safe and let him be okay."

He feels a peace—not so much like everything is going to be okay, as much as it is time to get some sleep.

"Ms. Finch, please come with me."

Cathy rises out of her chair and accompanies Dr. Hannaford to Andy's room.

Andy would look like he is sleeping if it wasn't for the tube in his mouth and several monitors hooked up to him with lots of wires.

"Is he going to be okay?" Cathy asks.

"It's too soon to know just yet. We will know shortly the extent of the complications and more about what to expect. Until he comes out of the coma, it's difficult to predict."

"How long does that take? I mean, he'll come out of the coma, right?" Cathy is feeling an overwhelming weight of fear, shock, and exhaustion.

Dr. Hannaford pauses for a moment, as he searches for the right words, for comforting words.

Then, placing his hand on Cathy's hand, he says, "We just don't know yet."

Wednesday

sixteen

ZACK FINALLY FALLS asleep after midnight.
    He enters a deep sleep, and then his dream comes back just before he's supposed to wake up. Zack is back in the game, still rounding first base. He looks up and finally sees the results of his hit. The ball slams into the top of the left-center field wall and ricochets toward center field.

Since the center fielder was committed toward running to the wall at left-center, the ball and the center fielder are like ships passing in the night. When the ball shoots past him, he cannot stop. The ball skips along the warning track, away from the center fielder.

Zack keeps pumping his arms. There will be no play

at second base. Should he take third? But what about the third base runner?

The runner who made his way from first base on Zack's hit is being waved in. If he scores, the game will be tied and his team will be guaranteed extra innings.

Zack arches his path toward right center field on his way to second, glancing momentarily at the center fielder, who has turned around and started running toward the ball as it bounces and continues to roll along the warning track.

Zack is nearing second with his eyes now on the third base coach.

The cheers are growing louder. The sound is like a roar of waters more than the voices of people.

The third base coach is not frantic like the first base coach. Perhaps that's because the base runner ahead of Zack is about to score, tying the game. Nonetheless, the third base coach is definitely waving him to third.

"Son, wake up," Maggie whispers to Zack.

"What Mom?" Zack says, not yet sure if he's on the ball field or in his bed.

"I just got a call from Andy's mom. Andy is not doing well. He is in a coma."

"What? That's crazy! A coma?"

Zack wishes that he was back in his dream, but this news fully awakens him.

"Do you want me to pick you up after school and take you to see him?" Maggie asks.

"Yeah. Of course. Thanks."

Breakfast is quiet.

When all the Towers gather, Peter leads them in a family prayer. "Lord, we ask that Your healing hand be upon Andy. We ask that You give wisdom and guidance to the doctors. Please heal Andy. Bring wholeness to his body as well as peace. Please give peace to Cathy. Lord, we love You and trust You. We pray this in Your name, amen."

The other family members added their "amens" as well.

During the drive to school, Peter does not encourage Emma to bless anyone. Rather, he asks that she continue to pray for Andy throughout the school day.

"I will, Daddy. Thanks for the ride." Emma runs off to Meyers Elementary with her Hurley backpack bouncing behind her with each step.

As they drive up to the junior high, Peter tells Tyler that he loves him and asks that he also pray for Andy today.

"I cannot believe what happened to Andy," Tyler says. "But, yeah, you bet I'll pray for him today. Bye, Dad . . . love you."

Tyler gets out of the SUV and meets up with Mike.

As Peter motors to North Valley High, Justin, sitting in the far back with Zack, asks what happened to Andy. He receives the *SparkNotes* version from Zack since they only have a few minutes before their drop-off.

As Peter pulls into their drop-off zone, he speaks up. "Hey, Justin. How did it go yesterday? I mean with blessing someone."

Peter notices in his rearview mirror that Zack has

perked up. *This might get interesting.*

"Mr. Towers, there was this guy that I've seen before but I've never said hi to him. He's kind of a loner. At any rate, I saw him in the hall and thought about what you said. It's not like I was trying to remember what you told me, but . . ."

"That's fine. Keep going," Peter said with a smile and positive affirmation.

"For some reason, I decided to walk over and say hi. So I did."

Peter sees that Justin shows a slight but nonetheless genuine smile.

"Good job, buddy. That's great to hear."

As the boys hop out of the SUV, Peter has some last words for Zack.

"Don't forget to keep Andy in your prayers," Peter says. "And when you visit him this afternoon, tell him you are praying for him. Even if it looks like he cannot hear you, talk to him. Pray for him . . . and be there for him."

"Thanks, Dad. I will."

———————

Word spreads quickly around North Valley about what happened to Andy drinking half a bottle of tequila, along with taking some Xanax, and how he is in bad straights. The entire school is buzzing about him.

Few people know of the coma. Brett does not even know until after first period.

"God, please heal Andy." Emma prays silently at her desk just before lunch.

Tyler asks to go to the bathroom during fourth period. As he walks down the hall, he offers the following prayer: "God, be with Andy and help him to get better. To come out of the coma and not be sick or anything. Thank you."

At lunch, Zack is happy to see Joel. He is still sitting on his rock, but it looks like Joel has shed another layer.

"Hey, Joel." Zack walks over to Joel's exclusive real estate.

"Wassup Towers?" Then Joel extends his hand.

Zack doesn't want to act surprised, but he is. He also thinks it's cool.

"I'm bumming out about Andy. I'll be seeing him at the hospital after school, but I'm having a hard time keeping my head into my classes today."

"I know, dude. Really crazy. Can't believe it. What are you going to do there?"

"You know, my dad told me I should talk to him, even if it looks like he cannot hear me. So I am going to talk to him, pray for him, and just sit around I guess."

"When you talk to him, tell him I said hi. Maybe that will wake him up."

Zack chuckles. *Joel cracking a joke? That was actually pretty funny.* Still smiling, Zack answers back, "You got it, Joel. And hey, see you around."

As Zack is starting to walk over to his table in the Quad, Joel calls out, "You want to go to The Point Saturday morning?"

Zack really enjoyed surfing with Joel, but his sore arms! A couple of days to recover sounds good.

"Absolutely," Zack confirms.

seventeen

ZACK STANDS IN the front of school at 3:03. Because of practices, games, or something else to do with sports, leaving school that early doesn't happen too often.

Seeing his mom pull up, Zack jogs at the same steady pace he uses when he gets a base on balls and makes his way to first.

"How you doing?" Maggie asks as her son pulls himself into the passenger seat.

"Today was tough. I've been praying for Andy and thinking about him all day."

"Well, I'm glad you're going to go see him. I called his mom. So far no progress. It should be good for him to have you there."

Maggie holds the steering wheel with her left hand and strokes Zack's hair with her right hand. On a typical day, she wouldn't reach over to touch him like a mom would with her eight-year-old son. But in the state of mind that Zack is in, she feels like he receives the comfort and is mature enough to accept it.

When they pull up to Memorial Hospital, Maggie says, "I'm going to pick up Ty and Emma and do a couple of errands. I'll come back in an hour and a half."

"Thanks, Mom. I appreciate the ride." Zack leans over to give his mother a kiss on the cheek.

Once Zack signs in and is confirmed that he is on the list of expected visitors, he receives the plastic visitor badge. He clips the badge to his Lacoste shirt, covering the little crocodile.

"Please wait here," the clerk instructs. "Ms. Finch and the escort will meet you shortly."

Once the two arrive, the escort—an elderly woman in her seventies—walks them toward the main elevators.

"Hi, Ms. Finch," Zack offers as he approaches her and offers a quick hug.

Cathy expresses appreciation with her eyes, but no words come out.

Man, she sure looks tired, Zack thinks.

The escort makes eye contact with Zack. "We'll take Elevator B together to the third floor. That's as far as I go. Then you and Ms. Finch will go to the check-in area immediately in front of the elevator as you step out.

At the desk, show them your visitor badge and ask to see Andrew Finch in room 336." The escort was, by all appearances, a volunteer.

God, please let me know what to say to Andy. I'm really scared about this, Zack prays silently so that the other people in the elevator could not hear him.

As the elevator opened, the ICU third-floor receptionist, sitting at her post, greets Cathy and Andy's classmate. Zack takes the lead as they approach the front desk.

"Um, hi. We're here to see Andy. I mean Andrew Finch. He's in room 336." Zack points at, and then taps, his visitor badge.

With a smile, the receptionist replies, "Ms. Finch knows the way. Just follow her through that door." She points to a set of blue double-doors that has a sign above the formidable entryway reading **Intensive Care Unit**. "You will see his room on the right, but make sure that his nurse knows that you are here."

Zack is already walking toward the blue doors when he thanks the receptionist.

Once inside the ICU, Zack finds a woman in her forties with shoulder-length red hair and a light blue hospital outfit. A stethoscope dangles from her neck.

"Welcome back, Cathy," the red-headed nurse says. "I see you brought a visitor."

"Zack is a friend from school," Ms. Finch says.

"Go on in, but depending on his vitals, I may have to ask you both to step out."

"Okay, thanks," Andrew's mother says.

Zack follows Ms. Finch into the room. Next to Andy's

bed is a complicated-looking system of monitors from which come unsettling alerts, sounds, and hums. Andy has tubes and wires coming from everywhere, monitoring everything. The constant beep-beep-beeps make Zack nervous.

Cathy beckons for Zack to move a chair closer to Andy's bed and sit next to her son. Zack moves warily and silently prays, *Lord, I need you now. I need you to be real to me and to Andy.*

"You all right in here?" The red-headed nurse pops her head in the room.

"Yes, ma'am," Zack says.

"Okay. Just let me know if you need me." The nurse disappears into the hallway.

Zack was startled by the interruption. Not exactly the "peace" he was praying for.

Then he hears the voice again.

You're doing the right thing. Just love him.

Zack is sure the large angelic being is speaking, which fills his heart with encouragement.

He looks around. That's when he feels the presence of someone other than Andy's mom in the room.

"Ashkah! I didn't think that I'd be seeing you again. At least not so soon," Zack quietly whispers.

"You're doing a good job. Pray for Andy," Ashkah gently requests.

"Lord, I ask . . ." Zack starts to pray.

"And put your hand on his shoulder," Ashkah instructs. Even though Ashkah has interjected, it does not interrupt the prayer.

Zack shoots a quick look at Ms. Finch to find her

reading a magazine. She is unaware of the activity occurring just feet away from her.

" . . . that You would please be here with us," Zack's prayer continues without missing a beat. "And touch Andy. Heal Andy. I ask you this, believing that You can heal him and trusting that You will. I pray this in the name of Jesus, amen."

Zack senses that Ashkah is still right next to him. Zack turns his head to his right and looks over his shoulder. Ashkah, with his light blond hair falling in front of his face, takes on a Tim Tebow-like end zone kneel with all his weight on one knee and head bowed. Zack hears him say, "Amen, and thank you Father."

Then Zack thinks he hears Ashkah say something that sounds like "Yahshua" or "Yahweh," then returning to speaking English.

"Thank you," the angelic being says. "You reign on high and are the Almighty, the Giver of Life, and the Redeemer. We praise Your holy name, amen."

Zack closes his eyes again. "Thank you, Lord. Thank you for being here and touching Andy. I love you, Lord, and praise You and thank you that Your love is filling this room. And filling me. And filling Andy."

Zack opens his eyes. Ashkah is standing next to him.

"Everything okay in here?" The red-headed nurse had popped her head in again.

"We're fine, thanks," Zack answers. He looks her in the eyes, but she registers no concern about the large Scandinavian-looking man standing next to him. The ICU nurse asks Cathy if she's okay and then departs as quickly as she entered.

She cannot see Ashkah says a soft voice speaking into Zack's heart. Zack thinks that it might be his thoughts . . . or maybe, just maybe, it is the still quiet voice of the Lord.

As the nurse closes the door behind her, Zack realizes that his hand is still on Andy's shoulder and has been for the entire time. Zack quickly looks around the room, but this time there's no Ashkah.

He directs his gaze at Andy, who seems to be breathing heavier, almost like a yawn, but without opening his mouth. Andy stirs.

"Ms. Finch! Look!" Zack utters with excitement but at a volume that is sensitive to being in the ICU wing of the hospital. Then, a bit more robust, he says, "I think Andy is moving."

Andy's head turns to the left, then slowly to the right. His shoulders seem to be trying to stretch.

Zack hustles to the door and spots the nurse in the hallway.

"Nurse, please come quickly!"

The red-headed nurse returns with Andy's chart in her hand. "Yes, what can I do for you?"

"Look." Zack points at Andy's head. Cathy jumps up and darts to her son's side.

"Oh, my!" the nurse blurts. She comes around Zack to have a closer look. "Yup, he's coming out. This is great news."

With that, the nurse departs the room and returns a minute later accompanied by Dr. Hannaford. The doctor and the nurse move purposefully to Andy's side.

"Well, this sure is unexpected," Dr. Hannaford

comments. He gives the red-headed nurse several instructions that Zack doesn't understand.

Looking at Zack, Dr. Hannaford says, "Well, you may have been just what Andy needed. I will let you stay as we continue to assess Andy's status, but depending on what develops, I may have to ask you both to step outside. Okay?"

"Sure. I really want to be here for him." Zack feels like he is one big ball of exhausted emotion. He is elated and spent at the same moment.

"Thank you, Lord," Zack whispers.

"How are you today, Andrew?" the nurse asks.

"Uh, where am I? What's up . . . um, hey Z."

Andy's voice is raspy from the tube that had been in his throat. "Oh, where's the big blond dude? He looked too manly to be wearing a dress. Was that a dress?"

"Don't be alarmed," Dr. Hannaford reassures Zack. "It's not uncommon for patients to experience hallucinations or dramatic memories of dreams when they awaken from a coma. You'll have to step outside for now, young man, but Cathy, you can stay." Dr. Hannaford's smile shows that he feels something special may be happening.

Zack knows Andy will be just fine.

"Hey, we'll talk about the big dude in the skirt later," Zack facetiously assures Andy.

Zack is smiling and wants to hug someone—anyone. His happiness is bursting at the seams as he walks out of the room.

At the dinner table that night, each Towers kid shares about when and how they prayed for Andy. The family also enjoyed the updates about Harold, Vickie, Justin, Joel, and the others.

The focus is heightened, though, when Zack shares about praying for Andy in the hospital room, how Ashkah was by his side, and that the angel even joined them in prayer. He doesn't share about Andy's just-out-of-the-coma questions regarding the large dude wearing a dress. That would be for another day.

The looks on Tyler and Emma's faces when they hear about Ashkah include mouths open and eyes wide, and it almost seems like they aren't even breathing. They absorb an amazing story about the supernatural.

To provide context, Zack fills them in about Ashkah's visit at North Valley on Monday and the vision that he experienced.

After several minutes of being stunned about the story of the visitation from Ashkah, the glimpse into a disastrous scenario, and the other miraculous events, Emma has a question.

"I wonder if Ashkah was at Meyer Elementary when Vickie and I prayed at the swings the other day," Emma says with a twinkle in her eye.

That brought a quick smile to each of the Towers . . . but it also got them wondering.

After more chatting about the angelic being who intersected with Zack's life, Peter steps away to get his Bible. When he returns, he unpacks several Scriptures that shed light on how God works and how His angels are ministering spirits that He deploys at His choosing and as needed.

Before the dinner time ends, Maggie describes how awesome it was to see Cathy at the hospital when she picked up Zack. "The joy on her face! You don't see that type of unrestrained happiness too often," she says.

With a celebratory feel in the air, everyone basks in the joy of the miracle that Andy and Cathy Finch received.

Maggie soaks in the moment and lets the beauty of the recovery resonate in her heart. She reminds herself that the last couple of days have been pretty interesting. What will tomorrow bring?

Maggie doesn't know, but she can't wait to find out.

Thursday

eighteen

THAT NIGHT, AS Zack sleeps, he finds himself back in the game.

Zack is rounding second and aware that the runner from first is within steps of scoring, tying the score and guaranteeing extra innings.

Will Zack be held up at third? Or will he be waved home?

The cheers and chants swell and grow louder. Dirt from the infield flies off his cleats with every step. His arms are pumping, and the balls of his feet are the only part of his stride making contact with the ground. He is in an all-out sprint. He knows that within a split second he will be given one of three instructions: slide, take third base standing up, or race for home and an inside-the-park home run.

The cheers are building, growing . . . Zack can physically feel the roaring cheers . . .

"It's double-play Thursday, and we will be playing back-to-back songs by your favorite artists. Coming up next is . . . "

Zack, lying on his stomach, swings his left arm back over his body and grasps his phone on the nightstand to turn off his alarm app.

Will he ever find out what happens?

———————

At the breakfast table, Zack kicks off the conversation. "Hey, Dad. How's the D.A.R.E. thing going?"

With the recent events that abruptly collided with his life, Zack is truly interested in what his dad is doing to create a relevant message.

Putting the sports page on his iPad aside, Peter replies, "Not sure. I thought I had my hands around a concept when we won the contract, but after the last couple days, I'm struck with how real this all is. Tell you what. This weekend I'll show you some story boards of our main ideas. You can let me know if anything looks good."

"That would be great, Dad. You know, I would like to look those over and let you know my thoughts. Maybe I can help make your campaign sound relatable and not preachy so kids will be willing to listen and not be turned off."

———————

Peter is smiling big on the inside and smiling even bigger on the outside in pure joy that his oldest son is "getting it" . . . that Zack is understanding the deceptive nature and dangers of drugs.

What a huge turnaround from earlier this week, Peter thinks. He allows the moment to sink in. A lot of transformation has taken place in just a few days.

"Hey, babe." Peter looks past Zack's left shoulder to Maggie, who stands at the counter packing lunches. "We have some great kids, don't you think?"

———————

"Well, everyone says that the kids are a lot like me."

Maggie is smiling but more like giggle-laughing. She, too, is amused, especially at her own humor, as she quickly glances at Tyler and Emma, who are finishing their bowls of breakfast cereal. In a few minutes, the four Towers will be leaving the house to attack the day. She mentally makes notes to be sure everyone has their backpacks, bagged lunches, gym bags, or whatever else they need.

Maggie lovingly sends off each Towers kid with hugs, kisses, and a reminder to "Make good choices." Peter just gets the hug and the kiss.

———————

As Peter is dropping off Emma, he looks in his rearview mirror and catches her smile. "Hey Emmer, you can make someone happy today. Be sure to reach out and be nice to someone."

"Okay, Dad. Love you."

Peter's next stop is Tyler's junior high. "Alright, Ty, today's a big day. Someone will be blessed by you reaching out. Just think—tonight at a dinner table, some kid may be telling his parents how Tyler Towers said hi to him and made his day."

"Well, I dunno about that, but I will bless someone today anyway," Tyler says. "Thanks."

Tyler is off and en route past the gym, on his way to the main building.

As the SUV leaves the curb, Zack, sitting next to Justin in the way back, is holding back a laugh. "Dad, don't do it. Just leave him alone."

"No, I can't leave Justin alone," Peter says.

"Sorry, buddy," Zack says, offering words of consolation to Justin.

Peter doesn't flinch. "What do you say Justin? Do you think that you can find someone to bless today, someone that you can reach out to and show some extra kindness?"

"Mr. Towers, I'll try. And, thanks for the ride. This has been quite a week so far."

"You're welcome, but we're not done yet. We still have another day to go!"

Then looking to Zack in his rearview mirror, Peter speaks up again. "Well, son, looks like you have a great day ahead of you. I hope all goes well with Joel, and remember to reach out to someone who needs acceptance, a smile, or something."

"You got it, Dad. And remember, you, too, can reach out to someone today," Zack replies with a smile and a slight chuckle.

Zack is glad that Dad knows he was teasing. *He's been a little more cool lately*, he thinks.

When Zack arrives at school, he greets the regulars and then spots Kelly. He gives her the usual hug and then fills her in about Andy.

"That's awesome—wow!" she says. "I have goose bumps just thinking about it. The outcome could have been bad. Like really bad."

"Yeah, like totally crazy."

Emma notices that when Vickie is putting her backpack on the hook in her cubby that the small zipper pouch holding her pencils is open. When Vickie tips her backpack, her pencils, erasers, and AirPods fall to the floor. Emma is quick to her feet and kneels alongside Vickie to help collect the articles strewn about the floor.

"Thanks," Vickie says with a big smile. "I can't believe I'm such a klutz."

"You're not at all, Vickie. Stuff like this happens all the time."

"Tyler," Harold calls out to his new friend.

"How you doing, bud?" Tyler offers a fist bump. The two are passing each other in the hallway, and Tyler thinks Harold looks pretty pumped.

"Good, man." Harold says. "See you later."

"You got it."

Tyler swings off his backpack and is getting ready to open his locker, which is next to Fluff's.

"Hey, Tyler, you gonna jam with us tomorrow night at my place?" Fluff asks as he opens his locker.

"Sounds good. You don't have a problem with Harold joining us, do you?"

Fluff shrugs his shoulders. "Um, no. That's fine."

Tyler notices that Fluff isn't enthusiastic, but at least he's on board. Then he turns and looks down the hallway until he spots Harold.

In a loud voice over the din of the other students, Tyler yells out, "Hey, Harold! You wanna join us for a little jam session tomorrow night? We're going to meet at Fluff's."

"Me?"

Tyler can tell that Harold looks surprised by the invitation.

Harold walks back to where Tyler and Fluff are. "Yeah, sure. I can bring my guitar, amp, and pedal. Uh, where do you live, Fluff?"

"Just meet us at lunch today and we'll set you up," Tyler says with an affirming smile.

— nineteen —

"HEY, ZACKIE. WHAT'S up?" Kelly is already at the usual Quad table. Lauren is also there along with Julie, Corey, and Brett. The buzz around the Quad is all about Andy and whether he will be okay.

"Hey, guys." Zack slips in and takes a seat.

In addition to the chatter about Andy, the rest of the conversations filling the Quad are about the typical stuff, mostly full of upbeat conversations . . . the agenda for this coming weekend, trending songs and videos, lame teachers, what's being binge-watched on Netflix, and other critical updates. Everyone is talking about whatever is important to them at the moment.

Zack looks over to the rock to check on Joel and catches an expression that looks like an invitation.

"Hey, Kelly. I'll be right back," Zack whispers as he makes his way to Joel's territory.

As Zack arrives at the rock, he asks Joel, "How's it going?"

"Pretty good, dude. Glad you came over here. I have something cool to share with you."

"Yeah. What's up?"

"Okay. So it goes like this. You know how you went to go talk to Andy even though you weren't sure he would be able to hear you?"

"How could I forget?" Zack interjects quickly so as not to break the cadence of Joel sharing whatever was on his mind.

"Well, it got me thinking."

"Yeah?"

"Well, just like you talking to Andy when he was out of it, I thought I should talk to my parents. I mean it's not like they really hear me anyway, but hey, maybe something would get through."

"And? "

"So last night I asked my mom and dad to hear me out. I mean, at first I totally wanted to just vent and then walk away, but it was crazy. They actually listened. They really heard me."

"That's nuts. Just like Andy!"

"Yep. Hundred percent. And they didn't cut me off or try to explain themselves or tell me how much I embarrass them. They listened. They even said something about me actually smiling more and not being so on edge . . . like they thought maybe something positive was going on with me."

"It's noticeable, dude."

"Yeah, I guess so. They were even pretty stoked that I reached out to Uncle Chuck. Then they offered to set up an appointment with a counselor at their church. I mean, he's supposed to be a cool guy who can relate to high school kids."

"That's awesome. I'm pumped to know that you have them on your side and listening. Very cool."

"Totally. And check this out . . . the guy that they want me to talk to has some rad tattoos. I checked out a picture of him on the church website, so at least I feel like I might not be fully judged."

"I can't believe how all this is happening for you."

"Yeah, I was feeling nervous about this whole 'talking to the parents' thing, but I just had a calm vibe, and it all worked out pretty well."

Zack notices Ashkah standing behind Joel. The angel's hand is resting on Joel's shoulder. Zack has more than just a hunch as to why Joel is feeling such calm.

When the lunch bell rings and they have to get moving to their fifth period classes, Zack sees himself in his mind's eye running to third.

He is remembering his dream again. He can see the look on the third baseman's face. Waiting for the relay. Usually Zack would expect a bluff, like the third baseman pretending that the ball is coming so that the runner will hesitate or maybe even slide instead of rounding the bag. But, no. The third baseman is unquestionably waiting and not bluffing. The third baseman's eyes are fixed deep into the outfield, looking for the ball to arrive.

Will Zack have to hold up at third, or will the coach wave him home?

Peter is excited to be working on the D.A.R.E. project and is confident that his recent experience will put him in the right strategic place for crafting a campaign that will resonate with kids . . . *and* his kids.

"Hey, Sue!" Maggie calls out.

The two moms find themselves in the Trader Joe's parking lot at the same time. Maggie figures they are both getting some necessities before the afternoon craziness hits with kids coming home, getting ready to go places, and either needing a ride somewhere or eating snacks with friends who sort of show up at the house after school.

"How are you doing?" Maggie is hoping for an update.

"Well, Greg has been open to counseling, and we really feel there is hope. We like the counselor we're considering. You know, something like a marriage therapist."

"I'm so happy for you two. Finding a good counselor isn't always easy, so when you find one that fits, that sure helps. Hey, Peter and I are praying for you guys. We love you and are excited that you're making this big investment in your marriage."

"Thanks. We're fighting with each other less, but the work does seem to take energy. But we're doing this for us and for the kids."

With that, Maggie and Sue make their way into Trader Joe's. As they each grab a red shopping cart, Maggie waves to Sue, grateful she ran into her.

I sure hope they make it.

Zack is in the boy's locker room, getting ready for a preseason baseball practice. As he sits on the bench facing his locker, tying up the laces on his baseball cleats, he wonders about his dream.

He is not overwhelmed. The dream does not invade him. Instead, he invites the thoughts. He sees himself running to third. He feels the adrenaline rush. He would have known if he was to go for home or stay on third if he had just had a couple more seconds before the alarm went off. He desperately wants to score on an inside-the-park grand slam to win the World Series. He wants to make a difference. To win for his team, for the fans, and for his city.

As Zack meets up with his teammates making their way to the ball field, he notices something out of the corner of his eye. It's Joel. He is sitting in the bleachers with a textbook open, reading and studying. He must feel like he's in a safe place. He's comfortable being near Zack.

Zack understands Joel in this one moment, in the span of a second. But it's weird because it feels like minutes have passed. Zack's mind and spirit are suspended from natural time, and somehow Zack understands stuff that ordinarily ought to be explained. That ought to take time to absorb. But in one single instant, he understands more about Joel. The Joel he remembers from sixth grade is re-emerging.

Zack makes eye contact with him and offers a head nod and smile. He notices that Joel responds with a slight, almost noticeable smile. His body language says, *Hey Zack, I'm good. Really, I'm good just hanging out here.*

At dinner that night, Peter is eager to catch up with the Towers' clan. He starts off with: "So, who blessed who today? Tell us about it."

It doesn't take long for the dinner conversation to be in full force.

Maggie asks Zack how his first preseason baseball practice goes.

"We did the usual. We loosened up our arms, then a couple of the coaches threw batting practice. Then we did infield while the outfielders practiced catching fly balls. Our next practice is Thursday, and then we start practicing Monday through Friday until the season starts."

After dinner, Maggie insists that Zack clean up his room. A few days' worth of pants, shirts, boxers, and socks are either on the floor, draping his desk chair, or hanging half out of his hamper. After putting his room in order, finishing his homework, and taking a shower, he calls it a night.

As Zack sleeps, he finds himself back in "The Dream."

Zack is closer to third base than he thought. The coach had already made it clear that Zack is to round third, run hard, and beat the throw to home plate. In an instant, it registers to him that the game is tied and he will either score the World Series-winning run, or his team will go into extra innings.

As he rounds third reaching his top speed and pumping his arms, the catcher is straddling home plate, mask off and glove at waist level. The pitcher McNamara, who is backing up home plate, stands behind the catcher as Zack charges in their direction. He is sprinting for home plate.

Zack is using all his resources. Every step is exhausting everything he has, but he will not and cannot stop. He has to score.

Zack can see the catcher raising his attention, eyes getting bigger. The ball must be getting closer. Zack wants to look but he knows that doing so may cause failure. He cannot afford to lose so much as half a step.

He is halfway down the base path, aware that the umpire is adjusting his position to make the call that can decide the World Series. Zack can hear the home team cheering him on. The whole world, it seems, wants him to win the game.

Zack spots his three teammates who have already scored. They're standing behind McNamara and waiting in intense anticipation. From where they are huddling, they are each yelling something different—"Down, down!" "Hit it!" or "Slide!"

Each means the same thing. The ball is coming in from the cut-off man, which means Zack has to slide at the optimal angle to avoid being tagged out.

As Zack nears home plate, his arms go up in the air as his right leg folds under him and tucks under his outstretched left leg. He lands on the ground in perfect slide position with the bottom of his right thigh bearing most of his weight. The catcher is reaching for the throw as Zack's lead foot is only a couple of feet from the plate.

Zack is sliding on the dirt. The catcher has the ball in his mitt and brushes the glove with the ball securely in the pocket toward Zack's lead leg. The intersection looks like the textbook definition of "simultaneous" to the unaided eye. With all the dirt flying, it's impossible for anyone in the stands to know if Zack is safe or out.

But it's not their call. That responsibility belongs to one person, and one person only. The home plate umpire.

"You're . . . " the umpire starts. "You're . . ."

Friday

twenty

"**A**NOTHER BEAUTIFUL MORNING, and your Friday music will be sure to get you going today . . ."

Zack's alarm app goes off about ten seconds sooner than he wants . . . again. Although he is stoked to have had the continuation of his dream all week—*How crazy is that!*—he is not happy to wake up like this. He really wants to score the winning run and to be safe at home. To feel the satisfaction of being the hero, of making history with a grand slam to win the World Series.

Does he beat the tag? Does his team win?

The breakfast table talk is mixed between Emma's plans for Vickie to join her for a sleep-over; Tyler meeting up at Fluff's for a guitar jam after dinner; Zack attending Kelly's volleyball match and his early Saturday morning surf session with Joel; Peter's anticipation about the new angle for the D.A.R.E. campaign; and Maggie's big meeting with the PTA.

An outsider would have thought that maybe no one was listening to each other, but among all the chatter, each Tower family member absorbs exactly what their ears need to hear.

Just before they leave, Zack looks like he is kissing his mom on the cheek, but he is whispering in her ear so that Tyler and Emma cannot hear.

"Can we have Kelly over for dinner tonight?" he asks.

Maggie smiles. She has always liked Kelly and is glad that Zack and Kelly were hanging out.

"Of course," she whispers with a smile.

After the three kids, Peter and Justin load into the SUV. A few blocks into the drive, the carpool banter is in full force. As they near Meyer Elementary, Peter starts in. "Emmer, love you baby, and be sure that you reach out and bless someone today. That is the most important thing you can do."

The words from Peter are the same, but he can tell that Emma knows he is sincere and that his words really mean something to her. Perhaps that's because his encouragement is offered with an authentic vibe and never comes across as robotic or nonchalant.

"Thanks, Dad. Love you too. I will be on the lookout." Emma skips away with her backpack, bouncing along with each hop and jump.

As the SUV pulls up to the junior high, Tyler beats his father to the punch.

"Dad, you know I'm totally excited about Harold, so I think I'll look for another person to reach out to today. In a weird sort of way, it's a cool thing to do."

"Ty, *you* are cool. I love you."

With Tyler gone, Peter figures that Justin knows what's coming.

"Well, Justin, we've had quite a week."

"Yes, Mr. Towers. It's been a trip."

"You're right, young man. This is the stuff that makes life great. This is the stuff that makes people great. Remember, you have been blessed, so be a blessing to others."

If Peter had to wager a guess, he would say that Justin, in his own way, is starting to get it.

Zack chimes in. "I was thinking that after surfing tomorrow morning, I would like to visit Andy. I got a text from him saying he'll be coming home soon, but it may be a little while until the doctor lets him go to school. With all he's been through, I bet that he would be a good person to check out your campaign stuff. You know, like to see if he thinks that it would help other kids."

"Great idea. You're on. When he's ready, ask him if he would be comfortable talking with me."

As Zack is getting ready to step out of the SUV,

Peter continues. "And be sure to bless someone today. Also, wish Kelly good luck with her match later on. Love you, son."

"Thanks, Dad. And remember . . . "

"I know, I know." Peter adopts the announcer/ commentator deep voice to mimic his son mimicking him when he says, "You bless someone too, Dad."

"That's right," Zack chuckles.

Peter thinks Zack is just like his mother, who likes to laugh at her own humor.

As Emma walks her way to class, she sees a boy sitting in the hallway outside of his classroom. He is undeniably popular and does not strike her as someone needing a blessing. But it just sort of happens. She says to herself, *I've never even said hi to him before, but everyone needs someone to be nice. The person does not have to look like he is hurting to get a blessing.*

"Hi!" Emma says in an excited voice that gets James' attention.

James is from the other fourth-grade class. She barely knows him because from kindergarten to fourth grade, Emma has never been in the same classroom with James. They've always had different teachers.

She finds James sitting in the same spot he always occupies before the door opens . . . on the floor in front of Mr. Rank's class, waiting for the first bell.

James, somewhat startled, looks up from the game he is playing on his phone. He is totally happy to be greeted with such enthusiasm . . . and by Emma Towers.

"Hi, Emma," James says with a smile in his eyes.

Emma feels tongue-tied. As she bounds away, she thinks, *Cool. He even knows my name.*

On his way toward the main building, Tyler passes the gym's dark wall. With the sun's rays hitting the wall at just the right angle . . . he catches a glimpse of the image of the tiger buried beneath the paint. Tyler's facial expression and demeanor make it clear that today will be a great day. He will look for someone to bless.

Tyler is smiling from his heart and wearing it on his face. He looks confident and strong.

As Zack strides through the hallway, he is thinking about what Justin said. *Yeah, this week has been a trip. Dad was right: we can bless people and really change their lives.*

"Hey, Zack. Come here a sec?" Kelly asks.

"Sure, what's up?" He greets Kelly with a customary hug.

"You going to watch my match today?"

"Of course. I love watching you play volleyball."

Zack is looking into Kelly's eyes and wants to tell her how much he likes her. Or maybe it's more than just "like."

Just then, Joel walks up to them. Zack knows that without a doubt Joel has turned a corner. The lack of piercings, necklace layers, black shirts in duplicate, black eyeliner, and black nail polish are a sure indicator that changes taking place on the inside are being reflected in his outward appearance. It's amazing what was hidden beneath the layers.

The troubled kid, who had his toes on the edge of a cliff and contemplated jumping, has clearly backed away. Not only that, but he's ready to rejoin life.

"Looking good, buddy," Zack greets Joel. "I like your new look."

"Yeah, I thought that I would tone it down a bit. Hey, how's Andy doing?"

"Do you want to know the real story? Dude, it was all you . . . your trick worked. I just told him you said hi and bam!—he jumped out of the coma."

They both laugh, but when Zack looks at Kelly, she wears an expression that says *And the funny part is—?*

"But really, he's doing great. I'm going to see him after we surf tomorrow, probably in the afternoon. Sounds like he may be back in school in about a week or so."

"Cool. That's awesome," Joel says.

Then, turning to Kelly, Joel says, "You looked good in the match the other day . . . the little I caught anyways."

"Thanks, Joel." Kelly smiles.

Zack is happy that she's part of the re-integration of the new Joel back into the real world.

Joel can't understand their kindness and forgiving nature. What he is experiencing is bizarre surrealness: the very people that he daydreamed about wiping off the face of the earth are the same people treating him with more than kindness . . . they are treating him with acceptance.

"Well, see you guys around," he says.

Joel is stoked, and he lets his smile be seen by whoever happens to look his way.

———————

Zack sees Joel more clearly. Zack used to see Joel as if he was viewing him from his dad's office conference room—with Joel on the outside. Anyone on the other side of the frosted glass was muted. They were blurred. It was impossible to see who they really are.

But Zack sees Joel differently now. He sees the real Joel.

———————

"Call on line four. It's your wife."

"Thanks, Sharon." Peter speaks into the intercom, which can be heard by his assistant outside his office door.

Peter punches the right key. "Good to hear from you, sweetie."

"How would you like a little Mexicana for lunch?"

"You are such a mind reader. Some Mexican food

is just what I need. You want to meet at Eduardo's?"

"How about at 12:15? Does that work for you?"

"See you then, love." Peter is smiling when he hangs up.

Then, with his eyes closed, he prays, "Lord, please give me your guidance and wisdom with this D.A.R.E. campaign. I'm excited to have this opportunity and ask that you would use me to reach the kids. Thank you, Lord."

twenty-One

A T LUNCH IN the Quad, Zack meets up with Kelly, Brett, Lauren, Julie, and Corey at their usual spot—their unofficially reserved table. There's a buzz in the air, and a few more kids gather to hear the update about Andy. Reese, Katie, Chris, and Claire join the huddle as Brett is unpacking the latest news.

Zack notices Joel sitting on his rock, scanning the Quad and looking at those entering the area. He isn't budging from his seat, nor does he look too threatening to be approached. When Joel makes eye contact with him, Zack lets out a little chuckle as they smile to each other.

"So, anyways," Brett continues, "my parents were

so upset, but just knowing that Andy will be alright makes it seem like my punishment is no biggie. I can handle being grounded the next month."

"You're pretty lucky things worked out," Kelly says.

"Yeah," Brett says. Then, turning to Zack, he says, "Dude, that must have been so weird to be in the room when Andy woke up from the coma."

Zack takes in a deep breath. "You know, Andy will have to tell you about it. But from my side, I mean, all I was doing was praying for him. My hand was on his shoulder, and he was looking like he was asleep—and then he woke up. But if you ask me, I'd say it was a real miracle. I can't tell you how glad I am that he will be okay."

"How crazy that drinking some tequila and taking a Xanax could do all that," Lauren says as she flutters and trembles.

Zack perceives that she is carrying a burden of guilt since she was the one who invited Andy to join them that night. Her eyes are beginning to tear up, and her voice quivers.

Kelly gets up and comes around to Lauren's side of the table and gives her a comforting, soothing hug. Zack has his hand on her shoulder—and he feels something strange yet familiar. He turns his head and sees Ashkah. The angelic being's strong hand is gently resting on his shoulder.

Zack takes a moment to soak it all in. He pauses, lowers his head, and whispers low enough so that those around cannot hear him. "Lord, I ask that you help Lauren to forgive herself. Lord, we know that You love her, and we praise you that Andy's going to be okay. But I ask that you help Lauren to receive your forgiveness, to experience Your presence, and to trust You from now on."

As Zack touches Lauren's shoulder, Ashkah is praying that the presence of God would flow to Lauren's heart and that she will receive a word of encouragement from the Lord.

When Zack is done, Lauren opens her eyes and looks around in bewilderment. "Wow, that was amazing," she says. "I feel such a peace right now, a sense of calm and feeling that—oh, I don't know—but like everything's going to be okay. It's like somehow I know that a miracle really did take place with Andy."

Zack feels a warmth on his shoulder and turns his head again to see a large bronze hand, that only his eyes can see, resting on his shoulder. He senses warmth running down his arm and out his fingers to Lauren's shoulder. He has no proof, but he is confident that the Lord has just touched Lauren in a new way. Perhaps she will never be the same again.

The conversation gets much lighter after that, and soon they are all talking about the kind of stuff that makes up the usual lunch table chatter.

After school, Zack sits with his friends in the North Valley bleachers as Kelly's team takes on a tough, skilled opponent from Harbor High. He notices Joel wander in, so he waves him over.

A few kids politely move around and rearrange their seats so that Joel can sit next to Zack.

Good to see you, Joel.

Hey, Joel, did you see that kill by Kelly?

Zack is happy that his crew is engaging Joel, making him feel welcome. Then, during a lull in the action, his concentration wanders.

The catcher isn't budging, so the throw from the cut-off man has to be on line. Zack hits the dirt and assumes a textbook slide position. The timing is so close that no one can possibly see if Zack's cleats reach home plate before the ball-in-the-mitt swooshes down to tag him. The fans are cheering as they await the outcome. His adrenaline is pumping, and his teammates are standing with mouths wide open. He can't hear himself think because the noise of the fans is so deafening.

Zack shakes his head, as if he is shaking cobwebs from his brain so that he can re-enter the real world. He does so just in time to see Kelly making a great play.

"Did you see the dig Kelly made?" Joel asks.

"Totally. She is awesome!" he replies, stoked that he regained awareness of his physical surroundings just in time. Then he quickly but briefly returns to his private thoughts.

I can't believe that I just saw and felt last night's dream in such a short period of time again. That's weird.

Joel stays until Kelly's team puts away Harbor High in the fourth set.

When the match is over, Joel nods to a few people and waves good-bye to Zack, then makes his way back to the main hallway. He needs to go to his locker and get his American History textbook before he goes home.

He has an odd sense to wait around his locker after he collects his textbooks for his homework that weekend. He somehow knows that he is supposed to stay where he is. He doesn't feel any particular reason but he knows that he's supposed to hang around and wait. But for what?

He does not see the large blond angelic being or hear him audibly whispering the instruction, "Stay here. In a moment, Corey will be coming down the hall. You have something that he needs. Just wait here." All Joel knows is that he has a sense to just chill and stay parked where he is for a moment.

Kelly showers and cleans up, then she, Zack, and Brett make their way from the gym to the hallway. There are only a few kids around this late in the day.

Zack notices Joel standing in front of his locker. He is with someone. Actually, he is talking with someone.

Corey opens up his locker two spots away from Joel. He is rummaging through his belongings and muttering, "I'll never be ready for that big test on Monday."

"The one in American History?" Joel asks.

"Yeah, that one. Wait a minute. You're in my class."
"Yeah, I am. I know I don't say much in class, but I rarely miss a question on our tests. I have a solid A. If you want, I can go over some things with you. It's the one class that I'm pretty good at. Want to meet tomorrow after I get back from a surf session? I think I could help you."

"You'd really do that for me? We barely know each other."

"Sure, why not? We can meet up at 11:00 at the Starbucks on Playa Vista."

"When did you get so good at American History?" Corey asks.

"Yeah, um, I don't know. But history seems to come easy to me."

"I never would have thought I'd be saying this, but sure, I could use the help. I'll meet you at Starbucks tomorrow. Thanks."

Zack walks over to the two of them. "Hi, guys. You saving the world here?"

"Nah," Joel offers. "We're talking about the big American History test on Monday. After we go surfing, Corey and I are going to meet to prep for the test. Just trying to help a fellow student bring home a good grade."

"Very cool," Zack says, arching an eyebrow. He didn't know that Joel was killing it in American History. This guy is full of surprises.

Just then, Zack feels a soothing warmth in the hallway. He looks around and sees Ashkah's hand on Joel's shoulder.

After this past week, nothing surprises him.

"So we're still on. Six o'clock at The Point," Zack says.

"Yeah, we got to get it when it's glassy. Can't wait to get into the water again."

Will wonders ever cease.

———

At the Towers' dinner table, Kelly is sitting next to Zack when he turns to his mother and says, "Hey, Mom. This lasagna is epic!"

Kelly closes her eyes to allow her senses to take in the delight of the amazing flavors in the lasagna. Then she opens them and says, "I never do this, Mrs. Towers, but I'm going to ask for seconds. Your lasagna is that good."

"Well, thank you for saying that," Maggie says. "Cooks appreciate every compliment." With that, Maggie makes eye contact with her three children, as if to say, *I like this gal!*

Zack picks up Kelly's plate to get her a second helping of lasagna from the kitchen.

As he walks away, the world feels right to him. It has been quite a school week, full of supernatural surprises and unexpected happenings. At the same time, he is feeling the weight of everything that happened the last five days and knows he will sleep well tonight.

Zack also knows that once he falls asleep, he will

find out if he beats the throw home.
    Does he score the winning run?
    Zack can't wait to find out.

Epilogue

NOW IT'S YOUR turn. Will you accept this challenge to be kind, loving, and caring to one another?

For the students reading this—be courageous! Take the bold step to bless someone today. Reach out to someone who needs you. Sometimes it will be obvious to know who you should reach out to and bless. At other times, listen to the quiet voice in your heart nudging you to say something or do something for a person in your path. Be alert for those opportunities. Today is your day to be a blessing to someone.

For the parents reading this story, let's become the role models. Show your kids what it looks like to live out this lifestyle.

In *The Blessing Effect*, Peter and Maggie Towers intentionally used the mornings to remind their kids to "do something bigger than themselves, reach out, and bless someone that day." Then the parents used their dinner table time to learn about the life-changing impacts their kids initiated. The important thing is to find a rhythm that works for you. Whether you are a single parent or two-parent home, carve out time to encourage and recognize your family's efforts to "reach out and care for others." There is no blessing too large or too small to applaud.

Lastly, sometimes the blessing that is being recognized is the one that you received. We all need kindness, so when your family is reflecting on how you blessed others, also be mindful of—and celebrate—when you are on the receiving end.

So, what do you say? Are you ready?

Let's change the world—one blessing at a time.

Robert K. Pozil

A Final Note

from ROBERT K. POZIL

IF YOU OR someone you know is experiencing thoughts of suicide, revenge, acting out in anger, depression, anxiety, loneliness, substance abuse, or other painful states, please know that there are people and resources available.

You are not alone.

Please reach out to a parent, pastor, teacher, coach, counselor, or other specially trained person. There are many organizations that are available to help you. An excellent resource is Teen Challenge. The organization can be reached at 417-581-2181.

Be sure to seek guidance, support, and love for the healing and blessing that awaits.

"You are the light of the world. A city built on a hill cannot be hid. No one after lighting a lamp puts it under the bushel basket, but on the lampstand, and it gives light to all the house. In the same way, let your light shine before others, so that they may see your good works and give glory to your Father in heaven."

MATTHEW 5:14-16 (NRSV)

———————

Do nothing out of selfish ambition or vain conceit. Rather, in humility value others above yourselves, not looking only to your own interests but also the interests of the others.

PHILIPPIANS 2: 3-4 (NIV)

Acknowledgments

THIS STORY WAS originally written for my kids fifteen years ago. Various scenes and episodes were inspired, in part, by events from my childhood and from events that took place with my kids and our family. With that in mind, first and foremost I want to thank my family. To my wife, Sue, my soul mate, best friend, and the one who journeyed with me for these past thirty-plus years. You are an amazing and talented woman. I love you, and thank you for being "My Girl!" To my four kids, Chris, Katie, Kelly, and Claire (CB): I love you. It's an honor that I get to be your dad.

We were living in New Jersey when this project began, so the neighborhood kids in Tenafly, New Jersey, who would hang around with our clan, also played a role in the inspiration to write this story.

While living on the East Coast, our New York City church friends unknowingly inspired me. A special shout-out to the pastor of that church, Dan Stratton, who first invited me to help with the church's youth ministry.

When I moved my family back to Southern California at the end of 2006, a new set of folks played various roles in our lives, and unwittingly they helped to motivate the completion of this shelved project. Among those I would like to acknowledge:

- Mariners Church in Irvine, California
- our lovely "small group" of families that we gather with regularly throughout the year
- the amazing couples in our neighborhood Bible Study
- the guys I cycle with on Saturday mornings
- the Tuesday morning Men's Group that meets at my office
- and the vast array of folks who Sue and I are blessed to call "our friends."

A special thank you to two guys who have been especially impactful in my life, Claus Hecht and Dave Hataj. Although neither played an intentional role in this book project, at different times in my life each of them has played the part of brother, confidant, or counselor while inspiring me along the way.

Thank you to my extended families: Carol and Norman Auslander; Richard Pozil and Leah Michaels; Richard and Joanne Lappert; Bennett and Cloudy Pozil; Steve and Mary Hicks; Sheri Boone; Eddie and Lorin Michaels; Steve and Linda Lappert; and all the other wonderful family members that make up our clan.

Thanks to my creative director, Emily Morelli, for

the design work on this book.

A special thanks to my Astro Pak family, probably the best place that one can wish to work, along with its host of terrific team members. At my work family, I must make a special acknowledgment to Ken Verheyen. Ken is not only a mentor and role model, but it was Ken who introduced me to Mike Yorkey, my excellent editor who did an awesome job helping me through the many edits (and re-writes). Mike, your patience and guidance were invaluable. I'm grateful!

Finally, thank you to the Lord God Almighty, our Heavenly Father who loves each of us with an abundance of grace and mercy and always provides a path to Himself. God is good, and to Him be the glory!

About the Author

ROBERT POZIL, a husband, father, and executive, is from Southern California. Shortly after graduating from the University of California Irvine, he spent fifteen years living in Tenafly, New Jersey. During his time on the East Coast, Robert's work facilitated extensive international travel that provided him with exposure to a variety of cultures and a wealth of experience in the global marketplace.

Today, back in Orange County, Robert works at Astro Pak Corporation as the company's Chief Business Development Officer. Robert has a passion for teaching and leadership. For several years, he has provided support for youth and men's ministries at various organizations and churches.

Robert and his wife of thirty-one years, Sue, have four children—Chris, Katie (married to Reese Dickens), Kelly, and Claire. Robert and Sue make their home in Irvine, California.

Robert Pozil can be reached at by email at rpoz@cox.net, Facebook @Robert Pozil, and Instagram @robertpozil.

To learn more, please visit robertpozil.com.

Made in the USA
Monee, IL
02 August 2022